T0157257

REQUIEM OF LIGHT

REQUIEM OF LIGHT

CHAOS CHRONICLES

COLT HORN

authorHOUSE®

AuthorHouse™
1663 Liberty Drive
Bloomington, IN 47403
www.authorhouse.com
Phone: 1-800-839-8640

© 2012 by Colt Horn. All rights reserved.

No part of this book may be reproduced, stored in a retrieval system, or transmitted by any means without the written permission of the author.

Published by AuthorHouse   03/15/2012

ISBN: 978-1-4634-1884-7 (sc)
ISBN: 978-1-4634-1883-0 (e)

Library of Congress Control Number: 2011909590

Any people depicted in stock imagery provided by Thinkstock are models, and such images are being used for illustrative purposes only.
Certain stock imagery © Thinkstock.

This book is printed on acid-free paper.

Because of the dynamic nature of the Internet, any web addresses or links contained in this book may have changed since publication and may no longer be valid. The views expressed in this work are solely those of the author and do not necessarily reflect the views of the publisher, and the publisher hereby disclaims any responsibility for them.

CHAPTER 1

A New Problem

In such a time when I was king, I ruled a nation of powerful beasts, cunning people, and mighty dragons. I was King Dechur, the Oracle King. I had power and had risen from peasantry and had slain the Tyrant God Myhuevrus. I was a prideful and caring king, to which all creatures and beings of my kingdom obeyed. But this story isn't about me. It is a story of two young lads and a lass whom I met 3 nights before my death by the traitor Gahryn. These are my last words for the memory of my kingdom and the heroes who defended it. May one day someone will find this spirit journal and spread the truth of this kingdom's origins.

"Atlas Penelope, you and Gahryn both know I hold no heir to the throne. So thus the decision is up to me to who ascends the throne. I specifically sta—," Two of my guards entered the room.

"Your Majesty, we have two prisoners here that have been accused of thievery, by Sir Fareld," said the leftwing guard. "That man is always causing trouble, if it weren't for his heroic deeds at the March of Durvyuria, I would have him strung up and whipped for insolence. Huuugh, oh well. What is it?"

Two boys were dragged in, followed by a housemaid I didn't recognize. The boys kept their heads low and the maid just watched them. "My lord," the maid curtsied.

"Hmmm," I said, "These two boys and you my dear, share destinies."

The maid blushed, "Is that so, My Lord?" "'Tis is true for I have seen it, though how they are linked eludes me . . . . Might I ask you your name?"

"Yes, My Lord, I am Lilah, Irea and Mescov's daughter."

I turned my attention to the lads presented to me. "What is the accusation in which you have been brought before me?" I ask.

The boy to my right spit to his side, and stated, "I hold no reason tell a lazy king like you!!" Before my personal assistant Penelope could say anything, the boy to the left kicked him. "Shut yer trap, Jason, He is the king and he has protected us from many dangers. Show him respect." This young lad spiked my interest. "And what is your name, young man? You have wise words and good morals, so why is it that the three of you are here?" Lilah blushed knowing that I saw how much she stared at this wise young lad. "My name is Dahrc, its spelled D-A-H-R-C, not D-A-R-K, I have no other name, but the reason we are brought here, Your Majesty, is because we were caught stealing from the royal pantry," the lad named Dahrc said.

"Why did you do such a task? Is food not a plenty for the villagers? Is there a problem that I am unaware of? For I am sure that these are not problems for my kingdom, such is my law and the Kingdom's wealth." I asked.

"No, My Lord, we did it merely because we have friends that dwell not within this kingdom, in a place where food is not a plenty, and is plagued by Soul Eaters. We could not ask our king for such a task, for fear of insolence. But the Soul Eaters threaten to annihilate the entire kingdom, and worse: invade ours. In truth sir our "friends" are foreign troops fighting the Soul Eaters, we do not steal much, just enough to be able to go without notice. You may think of our acts as treason, but I say this: Spare the others and do whatever you want with me. For it was my idea, I couldn't just stand there and let the soldiers be slaughtered," said the bold young man.

"Very well . . . . Soul Eaters, you say? What in the gods names are they doing out in the open? Are you sure that it is so? Soul Eaters are forest and cave dwellers, what would they be doing out in the open? But atlas, this would explain why I haven't heard from King Belimar for a while now."

"Please sir, show him mercy!!!" Lilah cried. "And you boy, Jason, is it? What do you have to say on this matter?"

"I have nothing to say to a king who does nothing to help those who suffer, I don't care for your lies!" the boy cried. Pity, he had such potential. "What manner of life befell you, my dear boy? For a man does not hold such a grudge unless he has reason." I said. The boy started to cry, and by the looks on the others faces, this was a sorrowful tale indeed.

Trumpets blared, which meant that Gahryn had returned from his latest crusade. "All hail, the Champion Gahryn!!" the squire announced. "Good evening my king. I see you have some trouble set before you, may I inquire?" asked Gahryn.

"Yes, yes, Gahryn, my old, good friend. These here have been caught stealing from the pantry, though they carry with them some troubling news."

"My Lord, what have you heard? I would not ask if it didn't seem important," inquired Gahryn

"Soul Eaters have nearly overwhelmed Granisti, our allied country. This would explain why we have not heard from Belimar for several months now. This truly has me troubled."

"Soul Eaters? But Your Majesty, Soul Eaters never come out of their forests and caves, why now?" asked Gahryn. "That would be the question, indeed, Gahryn," said Penelope.

"I have decided. We shall send a scouting force, to Granisti in order to see what is really going on. So as redemption for these three's crimes, they shall go too." I commanded, "Gahryn, Penelope, to my quarters, we have much to discuss. "Yes, My Lord," they all said in unison."

"Dismissed."

CHAPTER 2

March of Souls

"So, are you alright? Were you hurt? Those guardsmen can be really rough." Lilah expressed her concern. In truth Jason never expected the King to be . . . . so kind and generous. He had grown up thinking nothing but the hatred for the King. It had surprised him to find him as a gentle and kind hearted man. What Dahrc had said about him was true. But what of his family? What of his murdered mother and sister, and his lost father? If the king isn't to blame than who?

"He . . . . he wasn't what I expected him to be," Jason admitted truthfully.

Dahrc didn't say anything; he was too busy watching Lilah draw in the dirt. It was obvious how much they loved each other. A bit of jealousy flared within Jason, but he knew it was pointless.

He still wished however that he would find someone that he could share his soul with, but he hasn't met a girl like that yet, and he hated how Dahrc made it look easy.

Trumpets flared, a knight and his squire approached us. "No way . . . . it's Captain Erale, the Dragon Master!!!" said Dahrc. "Alright, I'm going to give it to you straight. You are to follow MY orders to the letter, say yes sir, no sir, and sorry sir. And you are not to interrupt me, or stray from the group, got it?" said Captain Erale, seriously. "Y-yes sir," Jason managed to say. "Now gear up, we leave immediately," said Captain Erale, as he galloped off.

"Oh, were going to hate this, I'm sure" said Dahrc. Jason agreed, for anyone who asks teenagers to join the army is certainly not in a good state of mind. But who can argue with the Oracle King? Jason thought he could, but after last night he wasn't so sure.

The march toward Bahyrnheit was tedious, Belimar's capital city within Granisti was a long trip and the commander refused to take short cuts that Jason, Dahrc, and Lilah had offered. "In war we march as men through every terrain!" Captain Erale had said. "But we aren't in a war," said Jason "At least not yet."

Dahrc didn't say anything, but for some reason Lilah found it horrendously funny.

The armor was a little too heavy for Jason, but he knew there was nothing he could do about it.

As they finally approach the once glorious and prosperous city, upon them a gruesome sight befell their eyes: The city had fallen, Soul Eaters had done the worst; men were either killed or enslaved, children were being corrupted into the Soul Eaters likeness, and the women . . . .

The soldiers cried out in shock, which turned to murmurs of rage. Captain Erale face was that of a statue, a stern and emotionless statue. "Arstas, you and these two will report back to King Dechur, and report the situation. The rest of you prepare for battle." Jason looked at the Captain wide eyed, the two others he selected were Dahrc and Lilah, but not him; Jason would be marching to battle, and only he knew just how terrifying the Soul Eaters truly were.

Captain Erale smiled a sinister smile, and said "CHARGE!!!!!"

CHAPTER 3

The Unthinkable

This couldn't be. Jason was staying? But that meant.... Lilah looked at Dahrc, "No .... We can't—" Lilah started to cry out, but Dahrc interrupted her, "We must return and warn the king, there is nothing we can do; besides Jason can take care of himself." He smiled.

But Lilah knew that smile all too well, he was lying and was terrified himself. "Let's go," said Arstas.

Terror and rage began to bubble within Lilah, how could this be happening? Jason was one of her only friends, if a little rash when it came to authority . . . . But now he was to fight in a hopeless battle, and Dahrc wasn't doing anything! Why? Why would the man she loved not care about his best friend? But she knew the answer, Dahrc DID want to go back, he did want to go back up there and tell Erale to send Jason with them. But how could he? It would only make things worse, and they could die.

She bit her lip. She told herself she would not cry until this was all over . . . .

Jason

The battle was not going well, for even with the element of surprise on their side, there were just too many. The armor was proving to be a drawback, it had to go. Three minutes later, Jason was back in the battle. As he checked numbers he counted only 32 men left out of the previous 120. The Soul Eaters were probably near a thousand.

As Jason fought, he thought of how people had complimented his sword ability, and of how it had shaped his life.

Thrust.

Slash.

Jump.

Rip.

Blood.

Jason reveled in the line of his work as he fell eight more Soul Eaters. And apparently killing one was an accomplishment. But as he battled, he searched for Captain Erale, he wasn't among the dead and he wasn't one of the five remaining which included Jason. Then he saw him. Jason's eyes grew wide as he saw Erale talking to two Soul Eaters. Jason sneaked away from the battle and hid in bush near Erale. Jason listened in. "Lord Gahryn sends his greetings, along with an offering of 120 souls. Are we still strong on our agreement?" said Erale. "Of course," said one of the Soul Eaters in its raspy voice, "We shall attack Durvyuria in three weeks, as soon as Gahryn has finished with the king." *Traitors. Despicable traitors! Must warn the others, but first . . . .* Jason thought. "Good tell King Gravre that we are ready. We shall be re—," said Erale. A sword sprouted from his chest, followed by the sound of ripping flesh as the sword pulled out. Erale's body fell to the ground revealing Jason standing with a look of hatred. "Kill him!!!" said the other Soul Eater.

Jason knew he was out numbered, for he was the only one left. Thought ceased after that, it was only instinct guiding Jason's blade. Weariness, worry, pain, all of it was dissolved in the slow mettle of Jason's mind. Time and reality seemed to freeze and the only thing moving was Jason's sword carving its way through, in a relentless slaughter. That's first time the Soul Eaters had ever shown fear, for none could stop him in his violent rampage. The fear was good.

Dahrc

Jason. His best friend. What had this world come to? Even Jason couldn't possibly survive that many Soul Eaters. *No. I must stay strong, for Lilah.* Dahrc thought. Worry was all he could think about no matter how hard he tried to shove it away. How could this happen? To distract himself Dahrc focused on his mission: report to the king about the siege of Bahyrnheit, and pray to the gods for a merciful death for Jason. The castle was just on the horizon.

"Dahrc, please say something, you've been silent for a while now. I'm worried too," said Lilah.

Damn. How stupid of me. I shouldn't have let her worry; after all if I show worry it will only make things worse, thought Dahrc. "I was just thinking of what we are going to say to King Dechur, I don't—," Dahrc stopped in mid-sentence, a sound of beating wings made him stop. *A dragon way out here? But Erale kept them away from kingdom lands, if one is this close to the kingdom than that means . . . . Erale is dead,* thought Dahrc. ". . . . out here? . . . . but that means . . . ." said Lilah. "We have to stop it. We can't let it come near the kingdom; cuz the only one able to stop it within the kingdom is the king. You, girl, aren't you a mage?" said Arstas.

"Y-yes," said Lilah, changing to her battle stance.

Dahrc backed away to give her room, for he knew it wasn't safe to be close when she started fighting.

Lilah

The thrill of battle was a strange concept to Lilah. Even though she had power, she hated using it. She couldn't understand what Dahrc or even Jason got out of it. For death meant the taking of life and the carnage of repetition. But even so this dragon had another thing coming. BOOM!! Lilah caused an explosion within the dragon's stomach, bringing it to the ground. "GRAAAAAAAAHHHHRRR" the dragon wasn't too happy about that, but Lilah didn't care. Lilah raised her hand, and upon bringing it down, unleashed an explosion that shook the very earth, and torched the endless sky. BWWWWOOOOOOOMMMMM!!!!!! That dragon didn't have a chance. Lilah smirked; *maybe this is what they mean,* thought Lilah. "Let's get going," said Dahrc, as if nothing happened. Two hours later they arrived at the castle.

CHAPTER 4

Traitor

"That was a disturbingly powerful force, for anything strong enough to cause such destruction is obviously a threat," said General Redds. "Redds, I assure you that whatever caused it, isn't a threat. I know that there's worry on the cause but I sense no da—," I started to say, when the sound of trumpets interrupted me. Shock covered my face as I saw three messengers, two of them I recognized as Lilah, and Dahrc, followed by a soldier.

"Bahyrnheit has fallen to the Soul Eaters," said Dahrc with a look of worry, though he tried to hide it. "Where are the others? Where is your friend?" I asked, for these questions could not be denied.

"Y-your Majesty, C-captain Erale was leading an assault on the city. He told us three to b-bring this message to you, but Jason . . . . He made Jason stay!!!" said Lilah, it seemed as if she was trying not to cry but inevitably failed on that matter, "And w-we think Erale is dead. A dragon was headed toward the city, where we intercepted it, and I dealt with it. Please!!! You must send someone to—," The boy named Dahrc grabbed her arm, and whispered something in her ear. The girl then went silent and clung to the boy.

"This is most troubling indeed, for Soul Eaters to be able to defeat the city of Bahyrnheit, they must have been in the thousands . . . . This arouses many questions . . ." I said.

"Wait, you're the one who caused that . . . explosion . . . ? You,—you must be a mage then." Said Redds.

She said nothing. "Enough! They look as if they need rest, we will finish this tomorrow!" I commanded.

"Yes, Your Majesty," they all said in unison.

Lilah

Anger and frustration endorsed Lilah, losing a friend like this was unfair. How could fate do this to her? And now everyone knew she was a mage, which meant either death or direct enslavement. Even if the king didn't want either to happen, he had no authority when it came to mages, the Aireni, a shady corporation that trained assassins, had full say on which would happen. Even though they had to reform themselves eight years ago when Jason left them, nothing has changed. She hated this; it was unfair, only Jason knew how to detect the Aireni and how to detect their traps. And now it was only her and Dahrc. Dahrc was a good leader and a clever one, but without Jason, Lilah was as good as dead. And that would mean Dahrc would have no one to be his family. *Get a hold of yourself*, Lilah thought, trying to comfort herself. But no matter how hard she tried, the tears could never stop.

Lilah cried herself to sleep that night, but dreamt of nothing.

Dahrc

Dahrc awoke to the sound of a trumpet, a trumpet that meant something was wrong. He quickly got dressed and hurried to the King's Hall. Upon arrival, Dahrc saw Lilah already awake standing next to the king. Gahryn was standing on the other side of King Dechur. "What is going on? Are we under attack? What is it?" Dahrc said, a bit worried. "No, a man approaches the city. He is armed and covered in blood," said King Dechur. "Perhaps it is Erale? Perhaps he is not dead after all," inquired Gahryn.

Dahrc looked to where the others were staring. Sure enough a distant figure of a man approached the city. And as he got closer, Dahrc's eyes widen. "Jason?" Dahrc said in astonishment. Lilah looked up, "Jason? Is he alive?" In a hurry Dahrc ran out of the castle and towards the city gates, Lilah not far behind. As the gate doors opened, sure enough, there stood Jason. Lilah ran over to Jason and gave him a big hug. Which obviously surprised Jason, and a flare of jealousy came over Dahrc as he shot her a questioning look.

She just stuck out her tongue.

But something about Jason disturbed Dahrc, instead of his normally detached look, there was only cold seriousness. "We must warn the king," said Jason. "What? What do you mean?" asked Dahrc.

"Erale was a traitor, working under Gahryn. Gahryn plans to kill the king," said Jason. "What??!! But how can that be? Gahryn would never betray our king . . . . would he?" this time it was Lilah's turn to speak.

"Where are they?" Jason said with a lethal tone. "King Dechur is with . . . . Oh no." Lilah darted for the castle, followed by Dharc and Jason.

Jason

"Halt!!!" said the castle guard. "We don't have time for that!!!" said Dahrc, grabbing his shirt, "Someone plans to kill the king!!!" The guards looked at each other and moved out of their way. They ran as fast as could. WHOMP! "OWW!!" Jason ran into Penelope head on, causing all of them to trip and stumble. "What are you doing? Are you—," Penelope started to rant. Jason's cold look made her stop. "Where is King Dechur?" Jason asks. "In his quarters, with Gahryn. Why—" Jason dashed ahead followed by Lilah and Dahrc.

Jason burst open the door, but it was too late. King Dechur was lying in a pool of blood. Gahryn was nowhere to be seen. Jason, Dahrc, and Lilah knelt before the dying body of the Oracle King. Jason noticed the others started to cry, but Jason was too wary to cry. He was so exhausted from his battle with the Soul Eaters, his long walk home, and all the running and excitement getting to the castle; that he no longer knew what he should feel.

"Y-you must . . . . r-run . . . . he plans . . . . to kill you three . . . . You must survive . . . You must . . . . ," The Oracle King's last words. Jason just stood there dumbfounded. What could he do? What should he do?

Just then the doors opened revealing Gahryn and several guards. "THERE!!! They killed the king!! Arrest them!! They shall be executed for this!!" said Gahryn. "W-what?!" said Lilah. Dahrc took action by pulling Lilah to the window, "Come on, Jason!" that snapped Jason out of his trance. He quickly ran and followed, parrying blades until he reached the window. With one smooth movement, Jason jumped, kicked off a guard's chest, and while in mid flip, grabbed Dahrc and Lilah, and disappeared as he went off the other side of the roof. As soon as Jason landed on the ground, they started running.

CHAPTER 5

Aireni

Lilah

They ran as hard as they could, and once they were outside the city, they kept running. They didn't stop until the city was no longer in view. Lilah rested on a log, and while she rested she cried. How could this happen? Why did this happen? "We . . . . We should keep moving . . . ." said Jason, "but at slower pace now." They walked for a little ways. She kept holding Dahrc's hand, to keep comfort, though it helped very little. Lilah couldn't think straight, too much had happened. THUMP.

Lilah and Dahrc stopped, and look back. Jason was lying face down on ground. "Jason!" Lilah and Dahrc said in unison. His eyes were closed and he was breathing hard. "He's okay he's just unconscious," said Dahrc, relieved. Lilah put her hand on his forehead. "He's burning up!!" This wasn't supposed to happen, the king shouldn't be dead, Gahryn shouldn't have been a traitor, the Soul Eaters should never have existed, and Jason can't be dying!! "What do we do? Where do we go? Dahrc, do something!!! We can't just let one of us die!!! We are a family, we have no one else!! I am not about to let one of my best friends die!!" Lilah said, confused and panicking. "We will do what we can do, keep going. There must be a village nearby. We must find it and get Jason to a healer," said Dahrc, obviously trying to think.

"Come on. We'll both carry him," said Dahrc. He slung one arm around his neck, and Lilah did the same with the other. Together they carried him on. Lilah was tired but she dared not stop, for if she did, they may not make it in time. Suddenly, a girl roughly around Lilah's age appeared in front of them.

"So, what do we have here? A charming boy, a mage, and a TRAITOR TO THE AIRENI!!!" said the woman. Lilah froze, wide eyed. This woman was one of the Aireni? Anger engulfed Lilah as she realized what this meant. Lilah raised one hand and let loose a powerful explosion. But the woman wasn't there.

"Behind you," said the woman. She turned to see the woman behind them, pulling out a terrifying yet beautiful scythe. Dahrc put Jason down and attacked. While outside of battle, Dahrc was wise and clever, but in battle he was a savage. His unique fighting style with short dual bladed battle axes was said to be like fighting an entire army, and felt like it too.

KLANG!!! KLANG, KANG, KLANG, KLANG, KLANG, KLANG, KANG, **KLANG**!!!! The last "klang" rang in Lilah's ear. Dahrc attacked with fierce, quick, and powerful strikes, but no matter how many times he striked, the woman blocked him. Then with the staff end of her scythe, she struck Dahrc in the chest, and he collapsed. "Dahrc!!" Lilah screamed. She raised her hand to summon her power but then . . . time seemed to slow as the woman jumped from where Lilah was targeting, and, to Lilah, slowly brought her scythe towards Lilah's face. There was nothing Lilah could do, she could only watch in terror as the scythe drew closer to its mark. And then . . . . KLANK!!!

There, right in front of her, stood Jason, blocking the scythe. "Dalia . . . what are you doing here?" asked Jason. *How can he still be standing*, thought Lilah, *when he is in such a poor state of health*? "Jason!! Don't you dare talk to me!!! You betrayed us!!! You slew our comrades!!! You betrayed us!!! You betrayed me!!!" said the woman who was Dalia. "We were friends, Dalia!! I did what I did because . . . . ," tears began to flow from Jason, "Because I found out what happened to your parents, Dalia. It wasn't bandits who killed your parents, it was THEM!!" Shock covered Dalia's face, "What? . . . . NO. You're lying!!! They raised us, protected us, and showed us how to harness our skill!! They wouldn't—," "Gabriel found out I knew, so he waited for you to go out on a mission, then he confronted me and tried to kill me, but he underestimated my ability. When I killed him, another assassin saw, and attacked me, and from that point everything went to hell.

Afterwards I knew if I stayed, they would kill you! So I ran . . . . ," said Jason.

Lilah was shocked, though she knew how he fled the Aireni, she never knew the reason. Now she knew. Whenever she asked, he always said, "It was for a friend." "If that's true, then why didn't you tell me?!!" Dalia demanded. She lunged with a flurry of blows with the scythe in ways Lilah never thought possible. But no matter what, she could not hit Jason. Despite his health, Jason parried, blocked, and struck blow for blow, quickly wearying down Dalia as if it was mere child's play. Lilah couldn't believe her eyes, how could Jason possibly still be able to fight, and with such skill? He looked like he could pass out any moment, and was sweating like a dog! Finally, THDSHEEN!!! Jason knocked the scythe from Dalia's hands, and using the hilt of his sword, knocked her out.

"Jason?" Lilah said worryingly. Jason just stood there, breathing hard, his back to Lilah. Dahrc finally got up, and he looked at Jason, then at Dalia. "Oww . . . . Jason? H-how did . . . ?" Dahrc stumbled over to Jason, "Jason?"

Jason collapsed.

Dahrc

They made camp that night. Dahrc raged through his memories. As he tied the woman named Dalia to a tree trunk, he thought about the first time he and Lilah met Jason. Lilah and him were traveling towards the city of Gullensburg to find shelter from a war that plagued the lands.

THUD. A kid his age ran into him, making them both fall over. The kid got up; "Stay away from me!" the kid yelled drawing his sword. "I wouldn't do that if I were you," Lilah had said, "Dahrc is a dangerous opponent."

The kid attacked anyway. Dahrc remembered that no matter how hard he swung or how many times or even where he struck, the kid, (Jason) either blocked, parried, or dodged. Finally Dahrc swung as hard as he could at the torso of the kid. Jason just jumped, flipped and slashed Dahrc across the face and landed on Dahrc's shoulders, making Dahrc lose balance and fall to the ground. The kid put his sword to Dahrc's throat and said, "So your name is Dahrc? Mine's Jason."

Dahrc chuckled to himself, he remembered how mad he was at Jason for giving him his scar, but no matter what Jason always won. But now things weren't as simple anymore. Jason is deathly sick, but still somehow managed to beat this woman who had also been able to beat Dahrc, which rarely anyone could. Who was this woman? The only reason Dahrc and Lilah decided to keep her alive was because Jason knew her and called her a *'friend'*.

She has a lot of questions to answer when she wakes, thought Dahrc.

CHAPTER 6

The Terror of the Truth.

Jason was still in bad shape when Lilah awoke, it was a miracle that he was still alive.

Dahrc and Lilah had alternated watch times in case Dalia woke up. Dahrc was still watching but, was obviously in deep thought. "You ok?" asked Lilah. Dahrc was slow to respond, "I honestly don't know, I mean, how did this happen? Why did this happen? And most importantly: What will happen? Lilah, I do not know what to do now. I just—I don't know." Lilah put her hand on Dahrc's hand and said, "We need to get Jason to a healer, but first we need to get some answers."

Two hours later, Dalia awoke. "Ugghh . . . . Wha? Oh crud," said Dalia. Dahrc put one of the blade ends of one of his axes on Dalia's throat. "Okay, here's the deal. I ask, you answer. If you do not answer or won't answer directly, we will cut out your tongue and swap it with one of yer thumbs," said Dahrc, seriously since it was no idle threat. Lilah knew that when it came to assassins, bandits, or tyrants, one should never threaten without the will to support it. Dalia's eyes widen, which was weird since, from what Lilah got from Jason, that assassins don't scare easily, if at all. "O-okay, hehah, let's not get hasty now, please," said Dalia, flinching at "please". Dahrc started off, "Who are you, and why did you attack us?" Dalia seemed to try and collect herself before answering; knowing what Lilah and Dahrc would do if she didn't answer right. "I-I am Dalia, Halea and M-Medron's d-daughter, I was s-sent to either e-eliminate Jason, or convince-vince him to come back."

"Stop stuttering! Talk clearly, before I lop an arm off!!" said Dahrc. For an assassin she was more terrified than anyone else Lilah had ever seen. And from the sound of her voice, it wasn't an act. The look on her face after Dahrc said that was that of a pale terrified ghoul. It was strange to see this after all that buster of self-confidence she had shown earlier.

Dahrc

"Next question, why does the Aireni want Jason back?" Dahrc asked, putting his axe closer to her neck. "Haven't you seen him fight? H-He is the best the Aireni ever had. His abilities are s-superhuman. He was beating masters at the age of three . . . ." Dalia flinched as Dahrc raised his axe and laid it leisurely on his shoulder. *What was she talking about? Jason hadn't ever said anything about this* . . . , Dahrc thought. Dalia continued to speak.

"I was sent to kill Jason cuz the Aireni don't want his abilities to fall into enemy hands, and if I failed, I was to o-offer to take him back. And I-I . . . . I . . . . I don't want to die!!!" Dalia said, starting to cry. Tears. Actual tears. Dahrc was utterly shocked. Tears from an assassin? Never in his life did he think he'd see the day when assassins cried. "Last question: How do you know Jason?" Dahrc knew that she was Aireni but he wanted to know everything about Jason's past. Dahrc was confused and furious at Jason. *How could he keep secrets from us?!!*, thought Dahrc. Dalia started to cry harder. "N-No!! Please don't make me answer that!! They will kill me!! Please!!!" "SHUT UP!!" Dahrc yelled, getting agitated, "For an assassin, you sure are a wimp!" "I know Jason because . . . . we were friends. A-And I-I met him during training. H-He was my opponent. I was sure I would beat him like all the others, cuz I knew how to wield the scythe better than anyone else, but he proved to be my superior. A-As w-we fought, I caught him with my scythe across his face, usually a wound such as that would make my opponent pause, but instead he . . . . returned the favor. Instead of killing me w-we became friends! Please, that's all I know!! Please, don't kill me!!" said Dalia. "Quit yer whining," Dahrc said, raising his axe. He smiled viciously. "**DAHRC!!!!**" Dahrc paused. "DAHRC!!! What are you doing?! She told us what we wanted to know!! You don't need to kill her!! What has gotten into you? This isn't like you!!" screamed Lilah.

Dahrc ignored her. He swung his axe. A hand appeared on Dahrc's arm, stopping him. At first

Dahrc thought it was Lilah, but when he looked, he saw Jason standing there, restraining him. "What are you doing, Dahrc?" Jason asked, staring unblinkingly into Dahrc's eyes. Dahrc lost it then, he threw his axes to the ground and tackled Jason. He started to punch Jason over and over. Dahrc kept hitting over and over but Jason wouldn't fight back. "FIGHT BACK!!!" he yelled, but Jason just took it. "FIGHT BACK!!!" Tears started to blur Dahrc's vision. When Dahrc got up, remorse barraged Dahrc as looked at Jason, who looked like a corpse but was still alive. "I-I'M SORRY!! It's just . . . . I DON'T KNOW WHAT TO DO ANYMORE!! THE KING'S DEAD, THE SOLDIERS OF BAHYRNHEIT ARE DEAD, AND THE SOUL EATERS ARE KILLING PEOPLE AS WE SPEAK!!! I just don't know anymore! I just don't know," said Dahrc, "But you!!! You kept secrets from us!! You swore you wouldn't but you lied!!! I don't need you. I trusted you but now . . . . now you deserve to die. Come on, Lilah, let's go." Lilah didn't move, she just looked at him with a hurt and scared look. "Lilah, come on!" "No." said Lilah.

"What?"

"I said no! I won't go with you; I don't even know you anymore."

Dahrc's face went cold. "Is that it? Fine. I don't need you! I DON'T NEED ANYONE!!"

And just like that, he walked away.

CHAPTER 7

Conflicting Thoughts

Lilah

"Dahrc," Lilah called, but no answer ever came. Lilah's heart felt as if it were shattered into a million pieces. But Lilah had to worry about more important things; Jason was sick and seriously hurt, and if Lilah didn't get him to a healer, he would surely die. *How can I possibly carry Jason by myself?* Lilah wondered. Then she looked at Dalia, who was still crying. Lilah thought about her situation, and unreassuringly walked over to Dalia. "Okay, listen, please, listen. Jason is dying. You said that you and him were friends, right? If that's true than help me, help Jason. If what you said is true, than if you go back to the Aireni, they will kill you. So please, help us," said Lilah. "I will help you get Jason to a healer but, that's it. After that we will never meet again." Dalia walked up to Jason, and kneeling down, kissed him. "Thank you," she said to Jason, "Thank you for showing me my foolishness." The words were so quiet that Lilah barely heard them. Then together they carried Jason towards the village on the horizon.

It took two hours to carry Jason to the village, and once they got there, they immediately requested a healer. They were then brought to a tent, and then put Jason on a mat; the healer went to work almost immediately. Dalia turned around and said, "This is goodbye," then she wasn't seen again. Lilah turned to the healer, "What is wrong with him? Will he be all right?" The healer looked at her and said, "He has Yellow Fever, and to make things worse, these wounds have weakened his immune system. Honestly I don't think he will survive. All I can do is ease his pain with ointment, and give him Rhedinol for his fever." Worry began to claw at Lilah. "But Jason is tough; he can make it! He has too . . . ." "Ah, just give him time then," the healer replied.

Lilah walked out of the tent, and nearly tripped on something. Lilah looked at what tripped her. It was Dalia's scythe. Covered in blood. Lilah looked around, but no one seemed to notice. There was a blood trail next to the scythe, so she followed it. A few minutes later she found Dalia. She was in a ditch, with strange markings carved into her skin; ritual suicide. After that Lilah didn't say much. For there was nothing to say. She could only hope for Jason's survival. And she dared not think about what had happened earlier.

Jason

Jason suddenly sat up. In doing so he scared the crap out of the strange man next to him, assumedly the healer. "Gods names!!! What the—oh, I see you've recovered." Jason got up, and started walking towards the tent exit. "Wait. Lie back down; you're not fully healed yet." Jason ignored him. "Hey!! I'm in charge here, so you listen to me when I am talking to you!" Jason turned and looked to him. Jason never did like authority. Jason walked out of the tent, but while he exited he flipped the healer off. As he took his first few steps, his foot hit something. Jason looked and recognized what it was: Dalia's scythe. In the Aireni, an assassin is to never part with his weapon. It is taught until it has become instinct. So for this to be here would mean that Dalia was dead and had preformed the Dihvr Ritual. Sadness whelmed within Jason as he looked upon Dalia's scythe. The reason why they became friends was because of Jason's skill and Dalia's ability to keep her humanity. She was the only assassin that retained her humanity when the killing of brothers, sisters, mothers, fathers, and friends began. And for that, he had admired her. He knew why she preformed the ritual. For she knew that no matter what, she was going to die. If an Aireni defects from the organization, they are hunted until killed. They did this when Jason defected, but eventually stopped when they couldn't provide the man power and skill to beat him. Jason stood there pondering his memories when the memories of what happened with Dahrc flooded his mind.

"*You kept secrets from us!!*" he had said, "*You swore you wouldn't but you lied!!!*" Jason looked at the blade of Dalia's scythe. The truth was only Jason knew about Dahrc's past. For at the time, Lilah was sleeping. "I need to tell you something, but first make a promise: No secrets okay?" Dahrc had said.

"Okay, I promise," Jason had replied. "Oh, good!! Okay I want to tell about my past, okay? You see, I grew up as an orphan, but I never lived in an orphanage. I ran away before anyone could get me. I grew up in the wilderness but I did sneak in and out of the cities for supplies and weapons. To defend myself from the wild, I trained myself in the way of the axe and I never trusted anyone. But word got out to a mercenary organization that an 8 yr old was defeating lions, tigers, and dragons and I was recruited. Three months later, on a mission I ran into Lilah and saved her, and then six months after that we met you. You two are my bestest friends in the whole world. To me, you are my family. Yer like a brother to me. But I have I question, am I yer brother?" "Yes. I would love to be your brother, as long as we watch each other's backs," Jason had replied. "And keep no secrets," said Dahrc. Jason nodded, "Yea, no secrets."

Jason put Dalia's scythe in a strap along his belt. "I'll keep it to remember you, Dalia." Jason looked around and saw Lilah passed out against the tent that Jason just exited. Jason walked over to her, "Lilah? Lilah. Lilah wake up," Jason said, feeling slightly tired himself. Lilah's eyes shot open, "J-Jason? Jason, you're awake!! It's been three days since we brought you here! I'm glad you're okay," Lilah said excitedly. Then she nearly tackled him and gave him another big hug, surprising Jason again.

"Oww, you're squeezing too hard on my neck . . . ." Jason said, trying to catch some air. She backed up, and looked away. Her face was blushed and her ears were red in embarrassment. "Lilah, we need to talk. The Soul Eaters plan to attack Durvyuria,"

CHAPTER 8

The Death of Us

Yraviro

It was not happy. It had seen what Death had done to its brethren. Death disguised himself as a normal human, but revealed himself for what he truly is: Death. His sword slaughtered its brethren. Death was all alone, his comrades had fallen, but He killed Erale. He killed the others. He was not human. He was Death. With its sword, it fought, but Death was better. It had retreated. It was named Yraviro. "Gravre, Its master, we have failed. We met with Erale at the human city as you asked. He gave the offering of a hundred-twenty souls, but unknown to us he hid Death within his ranks. Death alone killed our brethren; we four hundred are all that's left. Death wielded his sword like a plague and killed the others, he killed Erale too. What do you plan to do, master?" It bowed down, fearing its master's response. Its master looked upon it with harshness. "This death has struck against the wrong enemy. Death shall pay for its crime. Yraviro you are my witness, I hereby declare war on death. He shall pay for his crimes. Now rise, my darling, for your destiny, my dear wife, is to slay this death so that humans shall fear you, my precious Yraviro. Do not fear; for your failures shall be forgiven. Death is an enemy we shall defeat, but first the human kingdom of Durvyuria must fall," said Gravre. It had felt relieved, for it knew that females served upon a whim, no matter the rank. It bowed and walked to its home. *This is a strange time,* thought Yraviro, *this is the first time in history the Soul Eaters would leave their forests and caves for a war on humanity.*

It was fearful, for if its master would ever decide that it was not needed, it would die. It was taught at a young age that it was "it" not "she". It was to serve whatever master chose it. It was fortunate to be chosen by the king, or so it was told. It was to always serve, it had no rights, and all males are superior to females. It did not want to die. And now it was supposed to kill Death, an order that looked like an honor to the public but was actually an insult. Its master knew it was not skilled in battle. It knew that this was a punishment for its failure. It feared its master no longer saw it useful.

Soul Eaters and Humans never got along, though it was not because of looks, it was told, but rather of ideas. Even Humans have admitted to a Soul Eaters beauty. In history there was only one Human /Soul Eater couple. They both died tragically, which made a permanent split between the two, as restless as it was already was. It had constantly been complemented on its beauty, and it was true enough to attract the attention of its master. It hoped it would not die, it wanted to live. But in order to live, it would have to be an obedient servant.

It was later in the Eve. "Master, please forgive it for its failure!! It didn't count on Death being there!! Please!! Forgive it!!" It groveled at its master's feet. It felt only fear and sorrow from its failure. It waited for punishing words. "I do not take kindly to failure. You know this. But since you did not expect Death, your punishment shall be . . . . less severe," said Gravre. Its eyes opened wide, it knew what was to come next. Terror engulfed it, but it dared not resist. Its master raised his hand and touched the mark that was burned into its neck. The mark of Gravre. The mark began to glow and burn. Its master took away its will, and before it went blank, it let out a scream of agony.

It was wife. It was servant. It was slave. It was worthless. It regained its consciousness only to notice it had been locked in its room. It had been stripped of its belongings and would have to wait until its master called upon it. It could only cry; cry until it felt no more . . . .

CHAPTER 9

Travelers.

Jason

Jason and Lilah had been walking for some time now. They departed from the village in order to find Dahrc. They needed to all be there in order to stop the pending doom that awaited Durvyuria. Jason could only think of what had happened, of all the events that had occurred since they tried to rob the royal pantry. His emotions were no better. They were so jumbled up that he couldn't tell what he was feeling at the moment. He looked at his scythe. Dalia's scythe. He remembered all the missions they had and all the small little talks they had. Dalia was the only thing closest to a friend that he had in the Aireni. They kept each other safe from other assassins and constantly competed in countless things. *Another loss, death follows me, no matter where I go,* thought Jason, *if I don't protect my family and friends, there will be nothing left for me.* "Jason, are you okay? Don't worry we will find Dahrc, we have to. We are a family, we're HIS family. And right now he needs us whether he knows it or not," said Lilah.

"I seem to have a knack for messing things up, huh? It just no longer seems real to me anymore, none of it. I feel like I will wake up anytime now, and say 'that was a weird dream,' but the more this goes on, the worse it gets. I don't know where I'd be if friends like you, Dahrc, and even Dalia hadn't been there. And Dahrc . . . . I know why he was upset, I broke a promise. I kept a secret from him. But I didn't expect him to . . . . I didn't expect THIS to happen. It's all my fault," said Jason, never looking up. Lilah said nothing for a while, and then said something that he never thought was possible for her to say, "Jason . . . . what if you die? What if Dahrc dies? What if you both die? You two are all I have. Everyone else hates me. I know things are . . . . pretty messed up right now, but we need to keep going or else we won't make it." This was something Jason constantly thought about, but what worried him was that Lilah was thinking about it too.

"You know Soul Eaters are the weirdest things in this world," Jason said, changing the topic, "They are beautiful yet more savage than any animal. Plus they devour souls, though it ain't their only food source, strange right?" "I read a book once, on Soul Eater society. I know I don't want be a Soul Eater, cuz their women are pretty much slaves. Did you know they take this weird metal stick and burn these strange marks into the women's necks? And when the 'master' or the male that owns the woman, touches the mark, it saps the will of the woman. And I read it's really painful. Uuggghhh . . . . just creeps me out, thinking about it," said Lilah. They continued to talk until they reached a small village at the edge of the forest.

Lilah

When they arrived at the village, Lilah couldn't hold back her shock. All the villagers had been slaughtered. Man, woman, child, and even the animals. "What kind of beast did this?" Lilah said, breaking into tears. Jason didn't say anything, but Lilah notice how he adverted his eyes. Jason dashed off into the village and few minutes later, returned holding something in his hand. Lilah grew worried, cuz this time Jason had tears in his eyes. Lilah barely manage to say, ". . . . What? . . . . What did you find?" He held out his hand, revealing the object. Lilah froze; this couldn't be, for right there, in Jason's hand was Dahrc's amulet. The one he kept to remember his mother. ". . . . N-No . . . . No. NO! This can't be!!" she said. "Lilah, look around you. All these people were slain by some kind of blade, and how they died matches Dahrc's fighting style. I-I . . . ." said Jason. Lilah's heart shattered, everything was going wrong. *Dahrc did this? Dahrc, a killer? Dahrc, a monster? This can't be happening!! It can't be true!!!* Thought Lilah, but she knew in her heart that it was true. The evidence proved it thoroughly. Lilah looked at Jason. Jason had that look . . . the look of remembrance. The look of memories from the Aireni. The look of pain; the look of dread . . . . Lilah got the courage to do something she never thought would happen: she walked up to Jason and kissed him. She smiled to herself as Jason again looked surprised. Together they stood there, holding each other, mourning the loss of lives and the fate a friend.

Yraviro

It had waited for several hours. It could no longer cry. It was cold, it was scared, it was hungry, but it knew that its master would kill it, if it dared to flee from its prison. Its punishment wasn't over. It was not going to ever be free. For it had made Master mad. It had made the king mad. It did not want to die. Terror once again filled its soul as the door to its room unlocked and opened, revealing Gravre and two more of his servants. The marks on the servants were glowing, and their eyes were lifeless. They were will-less. "Restrain her. Her punishment isn't over," Gravre commanded. Terror consumed it. It fought back, but lost. In a matter of seconds they had it restrained. "Darling, you're such a fool. You know resistance only worsens your punishment. Ha ha ha ha," Gravre said, cruelly. Gravre then pulled out a rei rod, a rod used for burning holes into pelts of animal skins. It screamed as it was burned ten thousand times. Burned and terrified it then was forced to stick out its tongue, its master then took out his knife and carved his mark upon its tongue. He touched the mark on its tongue and it fell unconscious, tears still flowing.

Jason

As they left the village, they came across the body of a little girl. She was still reaching towards the forest as if she still had a chance. But Dahrc had made sure none survived. *I will make Dahrc pay for this*, thought Jason, *and then I'll accept whatever fate awaits me.* Jason felt confused; he didn't know what to think anymore. Lilah kissing him, Dahrc becoming a murderer, reality just didn't seem real. What was happening to them? Why was this happening to them? All these questions with little answers, but Jason wasn't a fool. He looked up and saw storm clouds in the distance. "We better make camp, or else we'll be walking in the rain," Jason chuckled. "Agreed."

They only gathered enough material for one tent, so Jason offered to sleep outside, but Lilah persisted otherwise. "There's nothing wrong with sharing a tent, besides, you just recovered from being sick, I don't need you to get sick again, now do I?" she had said. Lilah ended up being right; it stormed hard. But even with the storm the night was pleasant. A change most welcome to Jason after the revelations that this day had offered.

CHAPTER 10

Hunting Death

Lilah

Lilah awoke to find Jason still asleep, an unusual sight since Jason has always awoken before Dahrc and Lilah. As Lilah dressed, she pondered what they should do. *We must first find allies. Then amass an army to . . . . No, that won't work . . . . What of Gahryn? Even if they did build an army to defend Durvyuria, Gahryn would still be king, surrounded by guards, and could say anything he wanted about us*, Lilah thought. When Lilah looked outside, a sword was pressed to her throat. She let out a cry shock, but then a hand covered her mouth. They were surrounded by Soul Eaters. Luckily her cry was enough to wake Jason.

Jason burst out of the tent with his sword drawn, his eyes widened when he saw the Soul Eaters which then turned into a lethal, serious look. "The girl is with death!! Death is here!! Death shall pay for its crimes!!" said a female Soul Eater. "Yraviro, you are the one to kill him. We shall deal with the other human," said a male Soul Eater to the female. Jason looked at Lilah, and in one swift movement jumped over her and the Soul Eater restraining her, and cut the Soul Eater in half. With Lilah free, the battle had begun.

Yraviro

It had been ordered to find Death and kill him. If it did this, its master would be pleased. It found Death by accident. It came across a tent set up in the middle of a forest. It and its soldiers had to, of course, investigate. A female exited the tent first. Which Redroi restrained. But then Death revealed himself and, using skill Yraviro did not have, he killed Redroi, freeing the female. The female used strange powers; she caused explosions out of thin air, killing several Soul Eaters. *She must be a mage*, it thought. Death killed its brethren as easily as he did before. The mage female caused an explosion that killed the Soul Eaters next to it, and knocked it to the ground, wounded. Soon it was the only Soul Eater alive . . . Death approached, ready to strike his killing blow. It became terrified. "N-No, Please!!! It doesn't want to die!! It begs you, don't kill it!!!" it cried. The mage female spoke, "Jason, this Soul Eater is wounded, and there is no reason to kill her." Then Death, who was also called "Jason", spoke, "She refers to herself as 'it' . . . . How strange. Don't worry, we won't kill you. Why do you call yourself 'it' and not 'me' or 'I'? Don't worry, you're safe for now." It tried to flee, but its legs wouldn't obey, they only sent waves of pain that made it scream. "AAAAAAAAAAAHHHHH!!!!" It couldn't move; it was helpless; it was at the mercy of these humans. It didn't want to die.

Jason

"Don't worry, I know how to deal with broken bones, though the burn marks, you're gonna need a healer," said Jason, retrieving medic supplies from his pack. When Jason was talking about burn marks he was talking about her slightly scorched legs, an injury from Lilah's attack. But while he worked to fix her leg into a splint he notice odd linear burn marks across her body, by the look of the wounds they were at least a couple hours old, other words, still fresh. Then Lilah said, "By the Gods!! What happened to your tongue?!!! It's cut up and burnt . . . . kind of like the mark on your neck . . . ." "Lilah, careful, they ain't called Soul Eaters for nothing, you know. But seriously, she has several thousands of these burn marks, and they are still fresh . . . . What happened to you, Soul Eater?"

"I-it failed its master, it lost to death, it lost to Jason," she said, trying to pronounce Jason's name. Death . . . . She referred to him as Death. This thought disturb Jason, it disturbed him because, in a way, it was true. "They call you Death . . . . I guess they're as amazed as we are that you survived at Bahyrnheit. How did you survive, anyways? How did you cut away *thousands* of *Soul Eaters*? Defeating one in battle earns a person a treasure trove; But *thousands*? Jason, how? How did you do it?" Lilah asked. Jason looked down, how HAD he killed them? *What kind of beast have I become?* Jason thought. "In that moment, at Bahyrnheit, I just stopped. I stopped all thought, and then everything slowed down. I . . . . I felt calm, a calm I had never felt before, it was if my sword and I were one. Pain, worry, discomfort, fear, rage, anger, weariness, all of it was gone! I can't describe it, but at that moment, I was a god. It scares me to even think about it. Nothing touched me. I lost count of the bodies I killed after the first fifty. Wait . . . I remember some of them retreating, getting away . . . . I remember . . . . HER," Jason said, looking at the Soul Eater that he just bandaged.

Lilah

Lilah was shocked, Jason had felled nearly ten thousand Soul Eaters, and killed most of the ones that attacked today. Jason had done the impossible, not only did he defeat thousands of Soul Eaters, but afterwards he walked, never stopping, all the way to Durvyuria to warn them, then ran and helped them escape after Gahryn's betrayal, and ran several miles towards safety with her and Dahrc. And when he fell sick, he still had the strength to stand AND to fend off Dalia, making it look as if it were mere child's play, then he stopped Dahrc from killing Dalia, and took the beating instead, never fighting back. That he was still alive amazed Lilah, even now. By all rights, Jason shouldn't be alive. He shouldn't have been with her as they found the village, he shouldn't have been there when it rained, and she asked him to her tent. But yet, he was . . . .

The Soul Eater woman was even more terrified than Dalia was. She feared Jason, but Lilah didn't blame her, cuz she had seen him kill her own kind as if they were nothing. In a way, Lilah understood this, but there was more to her fear than just Jason. "N-no!! I-it failed!! Its Master's going to kill it!!! No, NO, NO, NO!!!! It doesn't want to DIE!!!!" she cried. "You're master? Why should you worry? He can't harm you here; he doesn't even know where you're at. Besides who is your 'master', and what is your name?" Jason asked, obviously thinking about something. Lilah felt confused, her heart was torn into a million pieces. She knew that if it weren't for Jason, she would have lost it. He was the only thing that kept her from losing her mind, and falling into more heartbreak. To distract herself she listened closely to what the Soul Eater would say. "I-its name is Yraviro . . . ." There was a pause as she continued to cry, then ". . . Its M-Master is named G-Gravre . . . ." Lilah didn't know who the Soul Eater was talking about. When she turned to Jason for help, she noticed that Jason's compassionate look turned cold, Lilah saw it was more than just recognition, it was deeper than that, she saw anger within his face, an anger that she had never seen before. "Your master's name is Gravre? The King of the Soul Eaters? You can return home, but not before taking a message to him. Tell him that the Aireni may no longer target him, but I will, for I was the best," said Jason. Then he helped her up, and with her splints in place he made her walk back. The Soul Eater cried the whole way back.

Jason then looked at Lilah, his mood changed. "We must head to Durvyuria. Now," he said. "What?!! But what about Gahryn? He's still there, you know. And he's probably looking for us, him and about a hundred thousand troops!!" Lilah protested. Jason just looked down and made an inaudible sigh. "Your right. I just don't know what to do now. Dahrc was the leader, not me. I don't know how to lead. All I know is how to fight; fight like a monster, a monster that you can't run from . . . ." Jason had that look again but this time it was sadness and remorse in his eyes. He looked like he was about to break, and that scared Lilah. Jason was the strong one. He could face anything. He was the one you wanted on your side if you ever in a tough spot. Dahrc was the one for thinking things through and could help if we things went wrong. But Jason never broke. He could take life head on. He could do things others wouldn't. So for him to break . . . . "You're not a monster! You're a friend. You are the one I can trust to always judge truthfully between right and wrong! Don't dwell in the past, please! Dahrc needs you! I need you." Lilah surprised herself with that last line, yet it was true. Jason looked at her and said, "You and Dahrc are all I have, just because one is lost doesn't mean we should forget about him. You are right. We are a family, so now we have to find Dahrc. We have to make things right." And together they walked again towards stormy clouds.

CHAPTER 11

The Terror Before Us

Yraviro

It cried as it walked back. Its legs burned from its wounds. The pain staggering its will. When she arrived at the entrance to the cave, it was escorted to the king, mocked at by guards for her failure. It was going to die for sure. Finally, it was presented to its master. "Yraviro, my dear, what happened? Where are the others? Are they dead?" its master asked. It couldn't take it anymore; it collapsed, it lost its will to stand. "Death surprised us again. He killed the others and spared it . . . Death traveled with a mage female who could command explosions. Death called himself 'Jason' and he only spared it to give you a message . . . ." It paused, it cried as pain surged through its legs, terrified of its master's wrath, it continued," 'The Aireni may no longer target you, but he will, for he was the best' that is Death's message! Please!—" it let a hoarse, animal cry as pain surged from its legs and overwhelmed it.

The king got up from his chair and walked up to its writhing body, and picked it up into his hands. "Summon the healers to my quarters, the rest of you are dismissed," its master commanded. It did the only thing it could do, it cried.

Jason

Thoughts about his mysterious past swarmed through Jason's mind. Who was his mom? Who was his father? How did they die? What were they like? What were their names? But most importantly: Why were they killed? All these questions, but no answers; this frustrated him, so he decided to think about something else. Lilah was his only comfort, though he wished he knew why she had suddenly changed her tune. It started to rain hard, so they had to stop and make camp.

While in the tent, Jason asked, "What about Dahrc? He's my best friend; I don't want to betray him more than I already have. I love you, Lilah, but what of Dahrc? I-I—" Lilah put her finger on his lips, "I know. I did love Dahrc. But that's changed now. You saw what he did to that village! He slaughtered all of them! Even the children! The poor, defenseless children!! How can I love a monster like that? He's different now. He killed the children . . . ." she said. Jason looked at her and said, "Well, then how can you love me? I am just as much as killer as Dahrc. I've killed many people, different ages . . . . How can you love me when I'm more of a monster than he is?" "Because, you aren't the boy from the Aireni, you aren't the same boy who would kill upon order. You aren't the boy who shows no mercy. You are Jason, the man who can do anything. The man who loves and protects his family, no matter what. You are the man who kills but also regrets. A monster doesn't regret. That's why there is hope. Hope for you, hope for Dahrc, and hope for me."

Penelope

Penelope hid herself in a corner, she wanted some time alone. She had to calm herself, to keep herself from crying, she thought of all the events that had happened. The king's death, Gahryn claiming the throne, the people cheering. She never suspected him of anything, so when Gahryn revealed himself to her for what he really is, a tyrant, she couldn't believe it. He had the people fooled, even now, with his kindness. Only those within the castle knew what he really was. He had cast a weird spell upon all of the guards, making them mindless and obedient servants. Then he killed the most of the servants. Then he captured Penelope and four other women, and branded them with strange markings. Branded them as his. Penelope tried to resist, but the markings sapped her will. But this was a week ago, it had only gotten worse. Penelope hated him, but no matter what, she couldn't stop the markings from sapping her will. He gave the women rags and told them to wear them. He crushed Penelope's golden rose hair ornament, and then forced the women to do all of the servant's work.

She was forced to perform on his very whim, but always she tried to fight it. But she couldn't anymore, for if she resisted anymore, he would kill the others. Hatred was the only thing that kept her from submission. She vowed that if she could ever get free, she'd kill him . . . . or die trying. But all she could do now was wait and pray for someone to come and free them.

Gahryn spent most of his time trying to find Jason, and the other two that were in his way. The Soul Eaters had reported to him that they have encountered them a few times and that one of them separated from the others and slaughtered an entire village. Penelope couldn't tell who was worse, Gahryn or the one who slaughtered an entire village. But what Penelope feared was when Gahryn wasn't thinking about Jason and his "co-conspirators". Then he would turn his attention towards them.

Lilah

As they walked, they had passed a squadron of slain soldiers, all of which had similar wounds as the people in the village. It was too much for Lilah, she couldn't bear to watch anymore. Jason was dull-eyed. His face was emotionless, a face with so much weariness and pain, that it stopped showing anything. They walked while it rained, never stopping to make camp. Lilah never once in her life pictured that this would happen. She always thought that she and Dahrc would be together no matter what, but now she just couldn't do that anymore. The pointless murders, the ruthless slaughter, all of this . . . . death.

The rain had started to fade when Lilah heard the screams in the distance. Jason and Lilah ran looked at each other. Then they ran towards the screams of agony and the sound of fighting. They ran to edge of a small cliff, which had a broad valley underneath. There they saw the worse: Dahrc was killing a group of travelers. Jason jumped and slid down the cliff and Lilah followed.

Jason

Jason quickly covered the ground between him and Dahrc, with Dahrc still not aware of his presence. "Dahrc!!" Jason said, showing his anger. Dahrc turned and glared. "You?! Graahh!!" Dahrc ignored the travelers and focused his attention on Jason. They clashed. **KLANG! KLANG KANG KLANG!!** "Jason!! You are a traitor!! You kept secrets from me. Before, I wasn't strong enough to beat you, but now, that has changed! I have realized my heritage!!! I know the name of my father!! And I know your father's name as well. Behold!! I am a son of Dihvr, the god of Carnage!!!" said Dahrc. Then Dahrc began to change. He grew wings of bladed metal, blood markings appeared on his skin, and his arms transformed into savage, inhuman claws. "I have discovered something glorious!! Can you not see this power? Don't you *desire* it? Hahahahahaha, you have this very same power . . . . brother." Jason stopped. "What?" he said confused. "Our mothers were different people, yes, this is true . . . . But our Father is the same person. You are a son of Dihvr as well!!!" Dahrc said while laughing. "Dahrc, stop this madness!! Please!!" Lilah cried. She ran towards him but Dahrc attacked her and sent her flying to the ground. Something in Jason clicked. Just as Dahrc was about to finish her, Jason ran, jumped, and delivered sixteen consecutive kicks before Dahrc could react, making Dahrc stagger back a few feet. "You'll pay for that, brother!!" said Dahrc. Lilah was covered in blood, Jason could see her wounds. "Jason?" asked Lilah. "Shh, I feel it again, Lilah, I feel the calm." Instinct again took over and all thought but one ceased, the thought was *Protect Lilah from Dahrc.*

His sword was no longer a weapon, but an instrument; every movement was a note in a melody. The melody of the opponent was powerful yet harsh, sound with no finesse. His was soft with coordinated notes and beautiful melody. Their melodies collided and formed a swift moving harmony, a sound of violent sorrow to which the ears of only Jason could hear. Such savageness did Dahrc hold with speed and furry, but yet he, even now, could not deny Jason's ability. Jason's sword was the only thing that protected Lilah. "How can you be this skillful? I have awakened!! You haven't!! We are alike, and I will NOT LOSE!!!" shouted Dahrc with obvious fury. "You think we are alike? You are wrong. There are differences between you and me, and THOSE are what matter. **I** never slaughtered an entire village, **I** never cleaved a young kitten in two, I never slew innocent children, **I** didn't behead little girls AND **I** WOULD NEVER HARM LILAH!!!!! And the Dahrc I knew wouldn't either . . . You aren't him. You aren't family. Families fight some times, yes but, never do they abandon each other and then try to harm the others. You aren't my family, you aren't my brother anymore," said Jason coldly, tears threatening to fall. Dahrc looked like he was punched in the gut, but then the look changed to a look of seething hatred.

Dahrc flew up, and with all his might, attacked Jason with everything. But Jason's calm kept pace. Then in a microsecond, barely visible to the eye, Jason switched positions and began to attack. In desperation Dahrc turned and launched a beam of dark energy towards Lilah. Jason saw this, and in one swift movement, he put himself in front of the attack. "AHHHHRRRGGHH!!" Jason collapsed on his knees. Everything went quiet. Then Jason felt a hand brush his arm and put a metal object into his hand, Jason turned around to see Lilah, bloodied and broken. He looked at his hand. Dahrc's Amulet, the only inheritance Dahrc had of his mother. "You dead yet, Jason?" Dahrc said viciously. Jason stood up. But instead of anger or worry, he only felt sorrow and pity.

He picked up his sword.

Dahrc attacked.

And Jason plunged his sword through Dahrc's heart.

"I was always alone . . ." said Dahrc. "You were never alone." Jason said, revealing the amulet. There was a look of awe in his eyes, and then he died. Jason picked up Lilah and walked away, crying.

CHAPTER 12

Torn

Lilah

Lilah recovered after a few days, Jason had taken care of her. Jason didn't talk nor sleep. He just stared at his hands as if they were that of a murderer's. Lilah got up and walked over to him, ankle still a little sore. She hugged him, to comfort him and herself. Dahrc was gone. And they were left broken. They remained like that till night fall, weariness finally got to them and they fell asleep.

Jason was awake when Lilah awoke. He was holding Dalia's scythe, polishing it. His face was depleted of emotion; though it was obvious he was in deep thought. Lilah didn't want to disturb him so she fetched breakfast instead, which wasn't hard since she was a mage. Roast rabbit and a couple of eggs was all she could find, but even so, it was a good meal. Jason didn't eat anything, for he was still polishing the scythe despite the fact it was spotless, so she brung him food. He stopped polishing as she drew near and said, "You know, it seems fate hates for me to have a family. First my mother and my sister, then Dalia, and Dahrc . . . . You're now all I have left . . . . Why does this keep happening? I don't want to lose anymore of my friends and family! But then I ask myself, 'Do I even deserve a family?' I killed my only brother. And I found out I'm the spawn of a violent and evil god, why should I deserve a family, I'm the spawn of evil, a monster . . . I-I'm . . . . I'm . . . .—" Lilah interrupted, ". . . . a good person who has lived on the dark side of life. I know you're pain, Jason. I'm an outcast, an unwanted freak with immense deadly power! You and Dahrc were the only things that kept safe, feel loved, feel normal, and feel joyful . . . . But now . . . . now everything is wrong!!! Dahrc's dead and the king's dead, and everybody keeps dying!! But I know that if we stop and give up, this will never end, and more than that, you are also the only thing *I* have, so please, we have to be strong . . ." Lilah went quiet, she didn't even believe in those words which she had spoken. Apparently Jason didn't buy it either, for he said, "Lilah. We share this pain, yet neither of us knows what to do anymore . . . . I . . . . I just don't know anymore, I don't know what to do, where to go, or why . . . All that's left for me in this life is you Lilah, and for you, I. All I know is this: Gahryn must pay for his sins, and when he does then shall everything be right again, I hope. I guess I should eat now."

Yraviro

It awoke to find itself within its master's quarters, its memories of its failures still fresh. It was bandaged and stiff, and it still couldn't walk. It pondered its pending fate, not knowing what its master might say, only fear and helplessness dwelled within it, for it knew not what to do. The door to its master's quarters opened a few moments later. The king stepped inside and looked upon it. Its master showed no signs of anger or disappointment, but rather a concerned and relieved look, which shocked it, but it dared not show it. "It is wounded, it can no longer serve its master . . . ." it said. Tears swelled in its eyes as it awaited its doom. But then its master said, "Do not think that my dear, for you have served me well, and still can. Though the healer said that you shall never be able to walk or run again, you can still serve me." He smiled gently, but it knew better. It knew what this meant, for what it was to become was worse than death. It was to become its master's possession, thus losing its title as wife. But again it was wrong. "You see, in order to heal you he needs an item I have called Anitium, the ore of the gods. I will give him this item, however, only if you promise to give me something in return," its master said. It didn't want to die, and if it wished to live, it had to serve. In order to serve, it needed to heal. "Anything, anything to live, please!!" it said. Its master smiled and said, "Just give me your soul." It froze. It's soul? Its master wanted its soul? But if it gave its master its soul it would permanently be bonded to him. She would never be able to escape. A choice worse than anything it could imagine. But with its choices few, it said the only thing it could, "Yes, its master . . ." He smiled and with great expertise, took its soul for himself.

Penelope

She was walking down the hall when she heard distant whispering. Being curious, she crept quietly towards the guest quarters, the door was cracked just enough for her to spy unnoticed. Gahryn was speaking to two cloaked figures. "I have ran the Aireni for almost 20 years now, and still, there has not been a single assassin as good as Jason. We must get him back. His skill is too precious to waste. But there is one assassin that has shown promise: Cynthia. Though she has a mental disorder she is easy to manipulate and has a silver tongue with a sharp knife to back it up. Her skill is quite exemplary. We will send her to capture the three. See to it immediately," said Gahryn. The two figures bowed and exited out of Penelope's sight. Gahryn turned to the door, so Penelope quickly moved on down the hall, for if she was caught spying, not only will she be punished but Gahryn's other servants as well.

She feared Gahryn's wrath as he turned his thoughts away from Jason and the others. She could never predict the tyrant's next move. Though she knew what was expected of her to do now. She hated Gahryn more than she ever thought possible. But the hatred seeped out of her as he activated the mark on her neck; she fell into a trance-like state, and then thought ceased.

Jason

It was a strange thing to wake up with Lilah in his arms. He never could get used to the idea, though strangely it comforted him; even after all that had happened there was still hope. Jason looked at Lilah and smiled, this would be a good day, which Jason welcomed greatly. Jason thought about him and Dahrc's final moments as friends, as brothers. He decided that he would have to stop at a two more places before he was ready to face Gahryn: Daterialiah, the home of the Gods, and Erinori Caves, the home of the Soul Eaters. But before he would go he had to ask Lilah one question: was SHE ready for this? Was she willing to go through this? He would ask her when she awoke.

Jason began to polish his sword, the sword which carried nearly all of his memories. The blade reflected Jason's image, and what Jason saw was himself, a man with a scar marked across his face, and was a little rugged but hardy enough to make it. A man without dreams. A soulless being with only one sole purpose, protect his loved ones. Jason stopped polishing for second; he looked at his hands again. Strong and callused, yet stable and finessed, these the hands that death commanded, with the blood of an evil god flowing through them. But yet, there was something else, too, he had his mother's blood as well, though what that meant, Jason couldn't tell. To calm himself, he went back to polishing his sword, and the flow of memories swept through him.

CHAPTER 13

A Task of Hunger

Bazil

It was quiet in the city. Durvyuria was a strange country; its own capital was named after it. But Bazil wasn't from Durvyuria; she was from Bahyrnheit, the capital in Granisti, where her mother and sisters lived. She decided that after her next job, she would return for a visit, and may even have some of her mother's cooking. But food was what was on her mind now; she hadn't done a job in several weeks, so she decided to look on the hit list that was on the city board. Being a lover of a full stomach, she always chose the highest paying job. "Let's see, 45,000 gold for Starlon, the Sharpshooter, 100,000 for Dari, a deserter . . . . And . . . . whoa . . . . 890,000 gold for anyone who can bring this man in, dead or alive. Jason, murderer of King Dechur. Well Jason, today's the day I get a full stomach for months on end!" Bazil said, with food on her mind. She took the flyer off the board and walked towards the city inn for some info.

The usual drunks and savages filled the inn, hooting and hollering like wild animals. Brazil walked up to her informant, Jarod, Mille and David's son. "So, who's the hit today, Bazil?" he said with his usual charisma. "A fellow named Jason; apparently he killed the late King Dechur. So, what do ya know?" Bazil replied. His face turned serious, a feature that rarely ever crossed his face, "Jason?" he lowered his voice, "The guy is a legend, he is a master of the sword who defected from the Aireni, after nearly wiping it out, and lived. I heard he fell ten thousand Soul Eaters in battle, single handedly, and returned with only minor cuts and bruises. He's a prodigy among prodigies." This shocked Bazil, for she knew who the Aireni were, and they had a right to be feared. So this one would be a challenge. But one question kept nagging at her, "How can that be true? Did he attack the Soul Eater's home or something? Soul Eaters don't normally amass in such large numbers, plus even one is hard to kill." His face grew distant, "You don't know? Bazil . . . . I'm so sorry . . . . The Soul Eaters . . . . they destroyed Bahyrnheit, and there were no survivors," Shock and terror overcame Bazil. She uttered a startled cry which silenced the room. "N-NO!! NO!! No, no, no, no, no, no, no, no, no, no, no, No!! No!! I-It can't be!!! NO!! You're lying!!! No!! No! No. No . . . ." This couldn't be true! How could this happen? Why did it happen? Anger suddenly began to stir deeply within her, "W-Why, why did this happen?" she demanded. Jarod looked at her and said, "If you want info there are only two people that could help you: A guy named Arstas who was sent to report to the king before the battle, and him, the guy you are hunting. He was the only survivor out of a scouting troop that tried to save the survivors. The rest died. It was a hundred-twenty to tens of thousands. The scouting force didn't stand a chance, but this Jason fellow, by himself, killed off most of them, making a remnant force of 400 retreat. The rest were dead. This is the guy who, you should seek out answers from, but be careful, if anyone sees you talking to him, you will be brought before the king for questioning, and possibly treason." "I got to go . . . . until we meet again . . . ." she said.

As exited the city gates, she mourned the loss of her family, and she promised, if they were still alive, she would find them, but first she needed to find Jason, this mysterious lad who had all of her answers. The last known location they were spotted at was somewhere in the Dlyai Forest. She would start her search there.

Lilah

She awoke to find Jason polishing his sword; he seemed calm, which put a smile on Lilah. But memories of Dahrc's death made it go away. Tears began to swell in her eyes, she wiped them before they could flow, because she knew if she started to cry, she wouldn't be able to stop. Jason paid no mind while she dressed; he was too focused on something else. After she finished, without even looking to check, he said, "I know what we have to do now, there are two places we need to visit before we take on Gahryn. First we need to go to Daterialiah, the land of the gods. And then we need to pay a visit to Erinori Caves, the Soul Eaters home. We both now know who my father is, so now I know who has the answers, maybe, just maybe, he could tell me who I am, who was my mother, and most importantly, what am I? Lilah, I need these answers, I've been searching for so long, and now I actually have a chance. Please . . ." Lilah looked into his eyes; she saw all the sorrow that he bore, all of his past and his guilt and his plea for mercy. "Of course, but answer this one question, why are we going to the Erinori Caves?" Lilah said gently. "Because Gravre and I have some unfinished business. He's still breathing," he said with that old feistiness of his, which made her smile. "Oh, is that it, now?" she said, jokingly. Despite what all had happened she desired nothing more than to kiss him at that moment, Jason had done many things for her, now she wished to return the favor. He deserved to find the answers he needed, and once he did, Gahryn would pay.

Yraviro

It no longer thought for itself, it no did know how, anymore. It still felt fear and terror, but its will was gone. Without a soul, a Soul Eater loses its will, but if a human loses its soul, then the human loses all of its emotions and may even die, but strangely it keeps its will. It could only wish that it had its soul, for now, it was will-less, aware, but will-less. It could not think about resisting, it could not think about what it wanted; it was at its master's mercy, for every time he activated his mark, instead of draining her will, it would drain its awareness until it was a living husk that obeyed its master's every order. This, it feared greatly. It did not sleep, for dreams were a sign of will and came from the soul, she could not speak unless it was an answer, or reply, for questions came from the will. It was no longer itself, it was worse than slave; it was its master's possession.

"My dear yraviro, you have a new mission. You shall seek out Death and capture him. He is wanted by the human king, Gahryn. Do not fail me," Gravre commanded. "Yes, master," it replied. It would have to bring him back, or else it would be killed for its many failures. It was going to die, no matter what; for it knew it could never defeat Death. It was not skilled. But it had no will, so thus it had to do its task. As it walked away, it cried for it was not going to survive this mission.

Jason

They had finished packing and were ready to go, but Jason paused for second. He felt the cool breeze that blew across the field, and thought about everything that had happened. He looked out into the horizon, towards Daterialiah. He would find the answers he needed, even if he had to beat it out of the gods.

He heard Lilah walk towards him and stop right next to him. "You ready?" she asked. Jason nodded, "Let's go." They walked for several hours, without a word, there was just too much on their minds. Finally Lilah said, "We should probably find something to eat." "Agreed," replied Jason. Jason sat down while Lilah went to go find food. Even though Lilah looked like she was okay, he knew she was still grieving for Dahrc. Whenever she thought he wasn't looking, she would look down with a grim face and such sorrow within her eyes. She didn't talk as much as she used too, but then again, Jason hadn't been the same either, since Dahrc's death. He couldn't ignore anything anymore. He would listen in to nature at night, when he fell into a trance which he could dream but still be aware of his surroundings. A moment when he was half way into the dream world, and half out, he would listen to the sounds of the night to calm his dreams, he felt like was a spirit when he dreamed, silent and mystical, yet aware and powerful. Lilah returned with a buck dragging behind her, dead. Jason helped skin it, and cut the meat. Lilah cooked it, and salted it. It was a good meal, and when they finished, it was about noon.

They continued to walk, but this time, to distract himself he said, "I never wanted to kill Dahrc. I still can't believe that I did it. I murdered my best friend, my own brother . . . . I-I . . . . I killed him . . . ." Jason looked down, for tears were swelling in his eyes and he didn't want Lilah to see him cry. Lilah put her hand on his and said, "It isn't your fault. Dahrc . . . . changed . . . ." She said the last part so softly, Jason barely heard it. He looked at her and saw that she was also trying not to cry. "It doesn't excuse what

I did! I could have found some way to help him!!"
Jason said, breaking down. Lilah looked at him with
a sadness that broke all illusions, and said, "No, you
couldn't. Something had happened to him. He was
beyond any help that we could ever offer. If you
had not have killed him, we would be dead, and
nothing would have change. I-It . . . . it . . . . it hurts
me to say this, but we both know this is true!!" Lilah
cried, and they stopped walking. Jason didn't know
what to say, and he hated himself for it. "I killed
him . . . ." Jason said distantly. Lilah looked at him,
forcing him to look her in the eye. "I . . . . I forgive
you . . . ." she said. Jason remained silent after that.
They continued to walk toward Daterialiah, in
hopes of finding answers . . . . and mercy.

CHAPTER 14

Blood Secrets

Lilah

Daterialiah neared and was only a mile away. The trees were gold with fruits that shown like jewels. The grass whispered silently, as if a great calm had spread from the heavens. The wind swayed the trees and plants, but damaged not a single speck of their magnificence. The mountains had bases which were lined with beauty, put had peaks which pointed into that which resembled black knives. Lilah felt calm, the beauty of it distracted her from her pain. So this is what it was like to be in the land of the gods. She was filled with awe, but returned her thoughts to the plan, when she noticed a figure waiting for them in the distance.

She grew wide eyed as she recognized the figure waiting for them. It was Dihvr, the God of Carnage. She drew closer to Jason as they approached him. **"Well, Hello there, son, Long time, no see, and I**

see you have brought a friend along as well, how quaint," said Dihvr. Lilah saw anger swell within Jason's features. "I want answers!!! WHO AM I?!! WHO WAS MY MOTHER?!!! AND FINALLY, **WHAT AM I?!!!**" Jason yelled, yearning for his answers. Dihvr chuckled, **"Who are you? Why, you're my son. You are Jason, the Prodigy of the Aireni. You are the perfection of carnage. Your brother was carnage with power, but you are better, you are more feared, you are the deadliest of them all, you are the finesse of carnage, you are my worthy son! Ha, ha, ha, ha, as for your mother, she was known as Jaya, a skilled warrior and beautiful young woman. Your sister was a wimpy "peaceful" type. You have your mother's hair you know, and you have her eyes . . . . And her sword."** Lilah looked at Jason's sheathed sword, shocked to find that it was his mother's. Apparently Jason was also shocked, for he said, "But the Aireni—," **"The Aireni found you with that sword. But before I can tell you that story, you must first know your mother's story. She was a descendant of the only Soul Eater/Human couple in history, making her 1/16 Soul Eater."** He paused for a moment. Jason was part Soul Eater? But he didn't have any resemblance to them . . . Dihvr continued to speak, **"When you were born, your eyes were multicolored, which each color had shown radiantly with irradecent shine. The villagers found out that you, your sister, and your mother were part Soul Eater, and ruthlessly slew your sister . . . . Hahahaha . . . . and they also slew your mother. Before she died she hid you with her sword, the foolish villagers became**

satisfied with their deaths and upon not finding you and they assumed you dead. The Aireni came the next day with orders to kill the villagers. Upon arriving at your home, they found you lying with your mother's sword. Naturally, they took you in and raised you." "What are you talking about?! My eyes are a dark green!! There's no way I'm part Soul Eater, I think I would have noticed by now!" Jason yelled. **"As you grew older, your eyes darkened into the color they are now, Hahaha, you know nothing! Now my little killer, you and your blade shall serve me, your father!"** Dihvr said, smiling viscously.

Jason

Jason drew his sword, anger engulfed him and he attacked Dihvr. Dihvr pulled out a circular disk-like blade, and the fight began. KLANG, SHING, WHRRRIIINNNNG, KLANG, KANG, KLANG!!! Dihvr spinned his blade at high intervals, forcing Jason to go on the defensive. Then, while Dihvr was in mid attack, Jason jumped through the Blade's hoop and stabbed Dihvr in the stomach, but Dihvr continued to attack. Jason used quick moves and strokes to maneuver around his father's attacks. There was no such thing as a head on attack, for Jason kept maneuvering, and on the occasion used his opponent's balance against him. Dihvr was finally showing frustration, but not much. He lunged at Jason and at that very moment, Jason jumped on Dihvr's blade and kicked his father in the face. Jason paused with his sword at the god's throat. "I don't serve you, and don't you ever, EVER, consider yourself my father!!" he yelled. "H-How did you know we were coming? You were waiting for us, as if you knew were we would be. How did you know?!" demanded Lilah. Dihvr chuckled, a horrid and cruel sound, **"I'm a god after all."** Then his body turned to a red mist and disappeared.

Jason stood there for a little while, but Lilah walked up to him and together they headed south, towards Erinori Caves.

Penelope

She awoke and found herself on the floor. Her immediate feeling was embarrassment, for she was unclothed, but she was alone. That feeling quickly turned to wrath, she could not stand this any longer, and she quickly dressed and kicked open the locked door. She searched for Gahryn, and did not find him until she saw him in war room. She stole a fire picker and a couple of knives from the kitchen, and returned to the war room. This time he noticed her. "Did I say you could come out? I think not," he said. "You son of a—!!!" she said, and she threw a knife at him. Quicker than the eye could see, Gahryn unsheathed one of his scythes and blocked it. He lunged at her with the scythe, and out of reaction she put the fire picker in front to protect her, but he had tricked her. He kicked her shins, knocking her off balance and grabbed her throat. "Now, now, what did I say about resistance, you'll be punished." He smiled. Then he touched the mark on her neck and everything went black.

CHAPTER 15

Disturbed

Penelope

She awoke, standing erect, looking at Gahryn, who was smiling. She glared and tried to say something, but then she felt something in her mouth, in an instant she realized what it was, a bone. They were in the dining hall. And on the table laid a half eaten woman who was still alive. There was blood on Penelope's hands, and when she saw her reflection in the mirror that was in the corner of the Dining Hall, there was blood all around her mouth. Penelope felt sick, and she tried to puke but her mouth wouldn't open. She started to scream, a muffled scream of shock, terror, and disgust. When she was at the point of tears, Gahryn said, "Enjoying your meal? Eat more." She tried to resist, but something sapped her will, but instead of blacking out, she was still aware. Terror consumed Penelope, and Gahryn said, "Eat." And against her will she ate, vigorously. She tried to stop, but Gahryn kept forcing her. The girl on the table screamed as she was eaten raw, she screamed until Penelope ate her heart. Penelope lost it then, but could do nothing, as Gahryn smiled and watched.

It was later in the eve, she had been locked in a storage closet, and the door was guarded from the outside. She puked and drank whatever she could but could not get the horrible taste out of her mouth, but the part that she hate the most, the part that disturbed her the most, was that she was still full. She laid on the ground and cried. Hatred was no more, Gahryn defeated that. She feared him more now; she wouldn't dare defy him again. She only hoped that someone would save her.

Jason

They walked without saying much. He was in deep thought, too much was happening. In the distance a figure approached. Jason recognized the stance the figure approached in and said, "Aireni, that person is from the Aireni." "Do you want me to—," Lilah started to say, but Jason said "Aireni, are good against mages for a reason, besides that person looks . . . . familiar . . ." the figure approached rapidly, and soon was in front of them. It was a woman, not much younger than he. His eyes widened as he recognized her. "Cynthia . . . ." Memories flashed through his mind, memories of his betrayal to the Aireni, the slaughtering of fellow assassins. The faces of the few he spared. She had been spared for he had disarmed her, and he couldn't bring himself to kill her, for she was naïve and innocent. She had a mental disorder that relied upon her knife. With the knife, she was fearless, assertive, smart mouthed, but without the knife in her hands, she was weak and easily controlled. It was almost like a dual personality, but it wasn't. "You are a traitor, Jason. I was there, you slaughtered the others. Wait, there are supposed to be three of you, where's the other one?" said Cynthia. "Dead," Jason said seriously. Lilah remained quiet, for she knew not to get involved; it would only make things difficult. "Oh well, I guess I'll just take you two in, Master Blade will be pleased none the less. This will be quick," said Cynthia. And she attacked.

Bazil

She was close, she knew it. She had followed a trail of scorch marks and footprints. She looked up when she heard the sound of distant battling. She raced up the hill and when she looked down she saw three people, two of them fighting. She recognized one of the fighters as her target, Jason. His opponent fought incredibly with a knife. Bazil decided to watch for a moment. Jason jumped, pointed his sword vertically downward and spun, the opponent, who was a young woman, went for the block, but Jason came down with a kick instead of a blade, and in three strokes of his sword, he disarmed her. Bazil expected a killing blow, or a sword to the neck, but instead, he picked up the knife, broke the blade, and chunked the two pieces in two different directions. The girl seemed to have changed, instead of boisterous or resiliency, she was completely submissive. Jason said a few words to the girl and she ran off. Bazil decided to jump in.

She jumped and landed a couple of feet in front of Jason. "Are you Jason?" she asked, and she drew her two swords. "I want answers!! Why are you the only survivor from Bahyrnheit? Why did the Soul Eaters attack it? How are you still breathing?!!" she demanded. Jason stood there for a moment and finally said, "I am Jason, and if you answers, then fine. I don't know why they attacked, but I know I survived due to my ability with the sword. If you want answers, it will take a long while to explain. I guess we'll make camp here, tonight."

Jason

It took till the evening for him to finish their story. The woman, who said she was named Bazil, looked at him wide-eyed. "So, the king, Gahryn, killed the previous king?! She's a mage and you're a prodigy of the sword. You found Bahyrnheit overwhelmed and . . . ." she trailed off. Obviously there was pain in those memories. Jason heard her stomach growl and she said "Can I come with you? I am good with dual wielding blades. Please? I need food! I haven't eaten in three days!! Please? I can help you with your mission . . ." Jason looked at Lilah and together they both said, "Sure." Maybe with a new acquaintance, their luck might change . . . . Jason hoped so, for he knew that he wouldn't be able to take anymore losses, not a single one.

Jason slept outside that night, Lilah didn't argue this time. He dreamt yet he was still aware of his surroundings. In his dreams; he wondered how he was able to do this, for he wasn't taught this, nor did it have anything to do with his heritage. He also dreamt of Dahrc and the day he killed him, but they never made any sense, they were jumbled memories mixed with a weird music that Jason had heard, yet there was no music that played. But then he remembered what the music was, it was the essence of their fight, and as the music played over in his mind, he felt that calm again.

In this calm, he thought of his plans for the next day; the Erinori Caves were only a half days' hike from their current location. His calm deepened, and suddenly he felt everything. All the soft noises that were beyond the human hearing suddenly became like a waterfall to Jason. He heard the heart beats of Lilah and Bazil, he heard the scuttle of the insects that traversed through hidden shadows, and he heard the breathing of every animal within a two mile radius and could pinpoint their exact location. But then something beautiful happened; every sound became a musical note, a hidden song of nature to which even his own breathing was attuned to. The music which came from each individual part of nature collided making a true harmony, the world itself was, unknowingly, singing. Jason was entranced by the harmony, and to add to it, he picked up his sword and added his melody. As he moved, the harmony became faster, but more elegant. All of time stood still, yet it moved faster than ever. There was not a noise in the night, yet this song rang loudly in his ears. He heard everything, yet nothing; he was lost within nature's song, yet aware of everything. He could now hear the melodies of everything in this world, the melodies of each of the gods, every animal, every beast, every human, elf, Soul Eater, and every motion, living or non; all of them collided with such beauty that words could never describe it.

All movement, even the slightest twitch was a part of this harmony. Every sound, even the softest breath, was joined in with irradecent beauty. There was no ugliness nor fault. Even the most atrocious of things radiated into this beauty, yet it harmed it not. Instead it made it more beautiful. True harmony, the only true essence of the world, this song gave Jason such a strong sense of peace that nothing could break it. The calm within him consumed him, until he finally stopped. A soft breath escaped from his lips. The song still playing, but no longer heard.

Lilah

Lilah awoke to a calm silence. She quickly dressed and as she exited the tent, she opened her eyes in shock, for Jason was doing the impossible; Dalia's scythe stood up, with blade on the ground and staff and hilt in the air, and on the hilt of the scythe was Jason's sword, balancing on its point at an adjacent angle and was spinning, and balancing on it with one hand on the hilt of the sword, was Jason, spinning with the sword. He had perfect balance, and more shockingly, was asleep. She watched in awe as he opened his eyes, and using his balancing hand that was on the hilt of his sword, jumped up, flipped and as he passed his sword on the way down, sheathed it, and kicked Dalia's scythe which rebounded off Bazil's tent and landed in his hand, which he then put it in through a loop in his belt. Lilah's mouth hung open, her eyes wide. Jason looked at her, "What?" he said, as if nothing had happened. "H-How did you do that?! You were spinning on your sword, which was spinning like a pin wheel around the hilt of Dalia's scythe with *PERFECT* balance, and you **WERE ASLEEP**!!! How in gods names did you do that?!!" Lilah exclaimed, a bit louder than she intended. Bazil came out of her tent. Jason smiled sheepishly.

"It was something I taught myself, and it took many years to master, I've done it before, y'all just haven't seen me do it before. You were asleep. I don't do it often, only when I need to think," Jason explained. "**THINK**?!!" Lilah said incredulously, "You were *ASLEEP*!!! You are telling me you can **BALANCE** like that, in your sleep, and you call that '***needing to think***'?!!!!" Lilah was bewildered, she knew Jason was skilled as an assassin, but she didn't know he could do anything like THAT. But she saw Jason staring at her unsuringly and she said, "I mean wow! It's just mind boggling, that's all. I mean I wake up to find you doing the impossible, while yer asleep! I'm just not used to it, that's all." Jason's face turned to an understanding look and then he smiled; a rare but gratifying feature to be seen on his face. "Alrighty, then. I guess we should eat and then get going, Gravre's throat isn't gonna slit itself, now is it?" Jason said, as if everything was fine in the world. Lilah smiled, while Brazil gave them a confused look but said nothing.

CHAPTER 16

Souls Collide

Bazil

As they approached the Erinori Caves, she thought they would take a switch towards stealth tactics, but Jason decided to go head on. "It's not much fun to sneak up on a Soul Eater, too much ego to deal with afterwards," he had said. Forty Soul Eaters stared at them as they approached. Jason and Brazil drew their weapons, but the other girl, Lilah, for some reason, did not carry any weapons and refused to accept one, nor sit the fight out. "Lilah, do you want the honors?" Jason said. Lilah nodded. Bazil looked at them confused. How was a disarmed girl going to fight forty Soul Eaters? BOOOOOMMMMMM!!!! That answered her question. The girl was a mage. All forty Soul Eaters lie dead, no chance at all. And so thus they entered the caves.

Jason

Their entrance was widely noticed by the Soul Eaters. But when they saw him, only a few attacked, the rest ran. Gravre had laced the caves with all kinds of traps, but they were obvious to Jason, and he easily disarmed them. Jason came to a room that was heavily guarded; an unusual four hundred Soul Eater force was guarding the door. Lilah took care of half of them within six attacks. Bazil was handling herself against three Soul Eaters, and Jason had already killed the rest. Bazil finished off her opponents and the three of them entered the room.

Jason saw a grand hall of thousands of Soul Eaters, in the back of the hall sat a throne, and on the throne sat Gravre. If Jason had to cut through these Soul Eaters to get to Gravre, he didn't mind. Though this thought gave him a chill when he realized how easily violence was to accept. "Jason, Hahahahahaha, I can't believe you were so kind to bring yourself to me. Gahryn has been looking for you. You are a fool, thinking you can barge in here and hope to come out alive." Gravre said in his arrogant tone. "I've done it before, Gravre. And this time, YOU are my mark. I don't care if that traitor, Gahryn, is looking for me. I did defect from the Aireni, but you are just too sick of a person for me to let live," Jason said, staring coldly at Gravre. "Hahahaha, Yraviro, my dear, take care of this trash that invades our home!!" commanded Gravre. "Yes, it's Master," said a voice. Jason turned to see who it was and stopped. It was the Soul Eater he had helped earlier, but she looked different, as if defeated. Jason knew what had happened. "You took her soul," said Jason, "Lilah, Bazil, get out of here. I'll meet you at the entrance." Lilah stared at him for a moment, and then said, "Okay." "Wait, what? Aren't we—," Bazil started to say but Lilah hurried her out. It was just Jason, Gravre, and tens of thousands of Soul Eaters.

Yraviro

Its death was imminent, it knew Jason was better, but its master had its soul, so it attacked. Its attacks were blocked and parried, and when he attacked it barely was able to block them. He was fast, swift, and moved like a ghost. It attacked with finesse, but not as fine as his. They clashed again, and it twirled to deliver a spinning slash, but he had already jumped in the air, and with the hilt of his sword, knocked it to the floor. Its sword skid far out of its reach. It was stunned, it could not move. It waited for the killing blow, but Jason did not perform it. "You will pay for that, Jason!! Soul Eaters, ATTACK!!!" growled its master in undefined rage. It watched as its brethren hopelessly attacked Jason. Jason looked different, this time there were no emotions upon his face, just like at the human capital Bahyrnheit. Nothing touched him. He became faster, so fast he was only seen in glimpses. A gruesome attack turned into a panicked retreat. Soon it was only its master and Jason. It still could not move. "Gravre, it's time for you to die," Jason said, while his eyes changed color. They turned into the color of the iridescent eyes which only the Soul Eaters had. A dark reddish aura began to emit from Jason as his face turned to an unearthly hatred. "What you do here, is disgusting. You have no sense of righteousness or justice. You abuse yer women and treat them as slaves. You have tortured and corrupted innocents. Your punishment is death!" seethed Jason. Grey withered wings sprouted from Jason. His hands became clawed, yet iridescent and finessed. Black markings surrounded his eyes. He became a beast of savage beauty. He was deadly on every feature, yet shown beauty which no human could match. It felt awe inspiring fear. His expression changed as well, a relaxed yet sinister-like stance with a calmness that brought chills to it. He still resembled his former self, but now he also shown his heritage, part god, part human, and more shockingly to it: Soul Eater. It let out a small gasp, but no one noticed. "Gravre, you shall not survive this. This will all be over shortly," Jason said, in a calm, chilling voice that seemed to grab one's soul, "Now, how should I kill you . . . ?" Gravre charged and shoved his hand into Jason's chest, "Your soul is mine, now!! Hahahahahaha!!" Gravre said viscously. But then Jason smiled. Gravre tugged as hard as he could but, he could not pull Jason's soul out, not even slightly. "Did you forget, Gravre? A Soul Eater can't steal another Soul Eater's soul without permission. And I got enough in me to say 'no'." Jason smiled, and he drew his sword, and with one stroke, decapitated its master. But the stroke was so powerful; it cut everything behind its master, everything that was in its path. Four other

Soul Eaters fell to the ground, beheaded. Jason then did something strange, he put his hand into its master's decapitated body and pulled out its soul, and reunited it with its soul.

Jason seemed surprised by his power, and when he looked in a mirror he jumped back a bit before realizing it was him. He shook his head and picked it up, and swung it over his shoulder. "Come on, let's get out of here," he said. As they walked out of the caves he turned back to normal, but not in time enough for his companions not to see.

Jason

"What was that?! Y-you looked different while you coming out!" exclaimed Lilah. Jason was unsure himself on what had happened. He knew he felt calm, but yet he also felt unbarring hatred for Gravre, and when the strange calm and his hatred collided, he felt powerful. "I don't know, I guess I somehow awakened, but trust me, I'm still me. Even I was shocked when it happened. Don't worry, I—," he paused, trying to see if his next words were true, then satisfied, "I'm still me. I'm still me." Bazil took notice of the Soul Eater slung over her shoulder, "Why did you bring her along? Is she special or something?" Lilah also looked at him puzzled. "She was a prisoner, a slave of Gravre. I looked for others before we came out, but the Soul Eaters had probably forced them to go with them. She is the only one I could find and save. Believe me, if I found more, there would be more," Jason said, seriously. He had never agreed with the Soul Eater's way of life, and he hated how they treated one another. But now Jason had to focus, he now only had one thing left to do: Kill Gahryn for murdering King Dechur.

They walked several miles towards the Echo Forests, the woods closest to Durvyuria. They made camp that night, with only two tents still, since Yraviro had no supplies. She still called herself it, but Jason and them would help with that, especially since Bazil thought it was annoying. They had a decent meal of deer and rabbit, and after eating, Bazil and Yraviro went to the tent that Bazil decided to share. Jason was just about to set out a mat on the ground where he would be sleeping, when Lilah said, "No, you and I need to talk, bring yer stuff to my tent. Besides, it will be freezing tonight." Jason knew she knew he was perfectly capable of keeping himself warm by just adjusting his mat, but he got the hint.

"What happened? Are you okay? What happened to you back there?" Lilah asked, worryingly, and put her arms around him. "I told you, I think I awakened. I don't know how but at that moment, right before me and Gravre were about to fight, I felt that strange calm and my deep hatred for Gahryn fuse together and then . . . ." he said, trailing off. "Awakened? But doesn't a demigod have to go through a ritual to awaken? I have never heard of self awakening without the Pelea Ritual. It's just so strange," said Lilah. "I know, I don't understand it either, I didn't even noticed I had changed until I saw my reflection. I know yer worried, so am I, but I just don't know what to think about it, but we need to focus. We still need to bring down Gahryn. This will require every ounce of skill just to get close to him, and if the legends about him are true, pray to the gods that we win," he said, though when he said gods, he was not including his father. Lilah went quiet for awhile, and then said, "Jason . . . . there is something I've been meaning to tell you since the past few months have gone by . . . . I'm pregnant . . ." Jason stared at her and sat down so suddenly, he nearly fell over. "Pregnant? Could it be Da—," she cut him off, "Despite what you might think Jason, Dahrc and I never had . . . ." Jason couldn't believe his ears. Tomorrow was his birthday, and he was already going to be a father. Jason tried to say something, but he just could not make words come out of his mouth. He took a moment to gather himself. "Whoa, this is just . . . Whoa! I-I don't know what to say, I'm happy, b-but—," Jason tried to say, but Lilah but her finger on his lips and said, "Don't worry about it, everything will be fine. Now let's get some sleep before it gets too cold outside." She kissed him, and blew out the candles.

CHAPTER 17

Birthday Boy Surprises

When Jason woke up, everyone else was already awake, an event that rarely ever happened. Jason was happy it was his birthday; he didn't care really, if anyone forgot because he was used to it. Eighteen years old already and he still had questions. Yesterday's drama swarmed in his mind, before he dismissed them and decided to just enjoy his birthday, remembered or not. He exited the tent to find a rather large feast being prepared. "It was going to be a surprise, but then again, no one really knows when you will wake up," said Lilah. Jason looked around. Yraviro was cooking and Bazil was trying to make sure she didn't burn the food. Yraviro, amazingly, had little experience in cooking, talking, and being a part of a group, instead of serving it. She seemed a little jumpy, as if afraid of them, but Jason hoped she could get through that. Bazil seemed perplexed, though spirited as ever. Jason avoided talking to her, but not because he hated her or anything, he just didn't want to take time and get to know her. He didn't know her, so why should he bother? It would only increase the risk of loss. Losing family and friends was something he just couldn't stomach.

Jason sat down and watched them cook, since Lilah wouldn't let him interfere. "It is yer birthday and I am not going to have you spoil it, just because you found out about the feast," she had said. Jason was polishing his sword when they called and said breakfast was ready. 'Breakfast' contained a lot of food such as roast deer, six spiced ducks, several eggs, dragon's tongue (Jason didn't know how they got that, for he was positive there were no dragons around, he would of heard), veritable vegetables, and a deflated cake, which Bazil explained, was just her luck at cooking.

Jason ate a bit, eating about half of the deer, but Bazil was obviously the hungriest of group. Jason had finished eating, and as he was about to get up, Lilah said, "Wait. You forgot something." Jason looked at her, puzzled. "Your birthday kiss," she said. Jason gave an exasperated sigh, and Lilah punched him in the arm. "Same old, Jason, you don't change much do you?" They both chuckled and kissed. That's when Bazil said, "Great, now we've got love birds, should we roast them up and serve them with the duck?" Jason and Lilah laughed, but Yraviro looked mortified. "She didn't mean it literally, she was just joking," said Lilah. "Was I?" said Bazil. "Not helping here," replied Lilah.

Lilah

Everything was alright; at least that is what Lilah wished it was. She did not tell the others about her pregnancy, and didn't want to them to know. She didn't want to be treated like a delicate object when she was perfectly capable of protecting herself. But Jason had to know, she knew him for too long to not tell him. Her dreams were a jumbled mess. She sometimes dreamt of Dahrc, sometimes of Jason, sometimes of Jason and her together, sometimes Dahrc and her, but the most frequent dream she had was one which Jason was split in two, one half was evil and malicious, the other gentle and remorseful. The evil Jason would over and over kill Dahrc, each time in a different way, the gentle one always would protect her and cry with her while they watched Dahrc die. She didn't like the dream, and each time it became weirder. She looked down at her stomach, and a wave of acceptance washed over her. She couldn't live in the past, only death and sorrow lived there, only the present and future held meaning. She smiled to herself, but she didn't know why. She sat down and began to rehearse the only song she ever knew. The one the old lady back at the farmlands in the village sung to her before she met Dahrc. It was her only lullaby.

Deep in the mountains, a deep beautiful forest awaits
For the one who is untouched by life's cruel fates
Deep in the mountains, lies a kingdom, with all its majesty

It lies in deep slumber for the centuries to come,
Its beauty lies deep in the road, the road of fantasy
It is you, oh dear baby blue, come oh, come dear
baby blue, come.

Deep in the mountains a terrible storm rains
A place where one's will does began to wane
Deep in the mountains, thunder strikes and
lightning sounds
The world as you know it is upside down.
Deep in the mountains the storm begins to burden
Those who follow shall not be so certain.
Deep in the mountains, where food is plenty and
dangers few,
Does your kingdom wait, wait for you
Oh dear baby blue, come oh, come dear baby blue.

Bazil

Night had fallen; they spent most of the day celebrating Jason's birthday. Bazil was not really tired but, she needed to think. She surprised herself when she looked into her own emotions and saw jealousy. It puzzled her deeply, for she only met them two days ago, what could she possibly be jealous about? And also, despite her vendetta against Soul Eaters, she felt a certain kinship with Yraviro; she figured it was because they shared pain, though what pain, she didn't know. She decided sleep would give her answers and so she lied in bed. Yraviro had cried herself to sleep, for her tears were still fresh upon her sleeping face. Bazil felt a calming chill run over her. Goosebumps appeared on her arm, and dreams welcomed her warmly.

Jason

Jason awoke to the sound of soldiers, they were close. It was still dark and when Jason exited the tent, it was too late, they had noticed them. He woke the others, and the others got ready for a fight, but Yraviro hid. Jason didn't mind it was only a band of 30 soldiers. There was only one woman with them, she followed them, and obeyed their commands. "Hey!!! Look, we've got some visitors!! And some of them are fine bodied too!!!" one of the soldiers hollered. Jason hated them already. In seconds they were surrounded. Jason drew his sword and attacked. He dispatched three of them before he heard Lilah scream. He turned and saw a soldier had snuck up and knocked her out. Jason swung his sword, but an unseen force flung his sword from his hand, and did the same with Bazil's weapons. Jason looked at the woman in realization. The woman was a mage. But before he could switch into his mage fighting mode, a sword was thrust into his stomach. As the sword was pulled out, Jason fell. The soldiers took off, carrying Lilah and Bazil, both unconscious. Jason was still alive, but the wound was enough to stun him for a few minutes. Yraviro came out of her hiding and started to cry, she obviously thought he was dead. He coughed once, spitting out blood, and got up. Yraviro looked surprised, but Jason didn't care, for he was focused on something else, Lilah was gone,

Gahryn's troops had taken her. But the soldiers didn't seem to have recognized them, for he knew he wouldn't be left there if they had. "LILAH!!" he yelled, as if that would bring her back. For several minutes that felt like hours, he knelt there, trying to think of what he should do.

All of sudden a yellow portal opened, and inside was complete darkness. Then a skeletal hand reached out and grabbed the side of the portal and slowly a skeleton with ragged clothes and two double bladed axes emerged. Jason stared in surprise, then muscle, organs, blood, and veins started to grow around the skeleton. Then flesh, then hair. Jason stood in complete shock as Dahrc stood right there in front of him, obviously just as surprised as Jason.

Dahrc

He was alive. It seemed impossible. His last memory was Jason killing him, and revealing Dahrc's mother's amulet to Dahrc. "D-Dahrc?!" Jason said, surprised. "Did you bring me back, Jason?" Dahrc asked, wondering how this happened. "No. I didn't." Jason looked fierce when he said that. Dahrc looked around, but he didn't see Lilah anywhere, but there was a Soul Eater standing right next to Jason. Jason acted as if she wasn't there, so Dahrc said, "Where is Lilah? And why is a Soul Eater standing right next to you?" "Lilah was taken by Gahryn's men along with Bazil," Jason said bitterly. "Bazil? Who's that? Never mind that, Lilah has been kidnapped?! We have to save her! I need to—," Dahrc tried to say more but Jason put his sword to Dahrc's throat and Dahrc stopped. "Who said she would want YOU to save her? Do you know what you did to her?! First, you slaughtered that village, EVERBODY was murdered by *YOU*!" said Jason. "But I—," Dahrc tried to say, but Jason interrupted him. "Lilah and I both saw that little girl you slaughtered. She was trying to escape from you, but you were merciless," Overwhelming remorse flooded Dahrc, but Jason wasn't finished, "Then you hurt Lilah. You almost killed her!! So why in the world should **I**—no,—**WE,** trust *YOU*?!!" Dahrc fell to his knees, "Oh gods . . . . What have I done? . . . . I . . . . I hurt Lilah, the woman I love . . . . What have I done?!" Tears overflowed and remorse and disgust of himself filled Dahrc. Jason paused for a second, and then he sheathed his sword. "There is another thing you need to know. Lilah is . . . . pregnant . . ." Dahrc looked at Jason with shock, "Pregnant?! Wha—b-but me and Lilah never—," "I know, the baby isn't yours . . . ." Jason's eyes darted away, as if the next words were too painful for him to say. "Then whose is it? Who is the father?!!" Dahrc demanded. Jason was silent for awhile and then, looking away, said, ". . . . Me . . . . I am the father." Dahrc stared at him, while a feeling of betrayal swelled within him, but then his remorse overcame it as he realized the truth; Lilah had forsaken him, for he had destroyed her heart. ". . . . Oh . . . ." The only thing Dahrc could do now is offer the only explanation for his actions, though he knew it didn't excuse him from his evil crimes. "Back at the castle, I touched King Dechur's blood. Anyone who touches the Oracle

King's blood is infected with madness. Neither you nor Lilah touched it. I found this out in the nether world, though I do not know who or what brought me back, nor why." Remorse kept him from saying more. Jason looked at him and said this, "I am not the one who should judge you, that is up to Lilah, so to get this over with, we must save her. You, me, and Yraviro can do this." Jason pointed at each of them when he said that. Dahrc looked at Yraviro, she seemed weak minded and fragile, and had not said a word since he met her. His guilt overcame his doubt and he said, "Yes, let's do this. Let's save Lilah and all the others that Gahryn has imprisoned." "Indeed, let's slit his throat and watch him bleed for his crimes!" Jason said fiercely. Dahrc was little unsettled by the vengeance in Jason's voice, but Dahrc did not disagree.

Penelope

Gahryn had bragged about the spell he put on her when she ate . . . . when she ate . . . . it was difficult to even think about it, for her stomach threatened to puke; the spell prevented her from spitting, puking or do anything but eat by closing her mouth. Of course he broke the spell when they were . . . . finished. Tears ran down her cheeks, for she was broken, Gahryn had made sure about that. She looked at her reflection. She could barely recognize herself; a broken girl in slave clothing and wild hair. She stared into her reflected eyes and only saw pain. There was no feistiness, no hatred, no anger, no joy, no pride, only pain and sorrow. Hope had fled.

Trumpets blared, a scouting party had returned. A squadron of 26 men and the enslaved mage returned with two people slung across their shoulders; both knocked out cold. They were in the royal courtroom; Penelope was there as well, for Gahryn wished it so. "Lieutenant Beyham, what is this? What happened? Where is the rest of your squadron? I sent you out with thirty men and you come back with four missing and two women slung over shoulders. Explain yourself," commanded Gahryn. Beyham, under his spell, said, "We found a campsite about six miles off, towards the outskirts of the forests, there three people camping there, two of which we thought were worthy of your eye. The woman over there," he pointed at the dirty blonde girl, "and the third camper fought back. Our mage disarmed them, but not after losing four men. It didn't take long to figure out that the other girl is also a mage," pointing at the auburn haired girl, "though she was subdued." "Take them to my quarters, and prepare the brands. Penelope, you are to be there as well." "Yes, Master," Penelope said, in a quivering voice.

CHAPTER 18

Broken Souls

Lilah

She awoke. She was slumped on an armored guard's shoulder. She was being carried to somewhere. She was in a castle. Her eyes widened, but she dared not move, she didn't know what these guards would do. She looked to her left and saw Bazil, who was also slung over a guard's shoulder. She hadn't awoken yet. They were taken to a room that had a royal mattress and two iron tables. They slung them onto the tables. "Ohw!" an unintentional sound of pain, but it let the guards know she was awake. The guards drew their swords and made them undress, Brazil now awake. Sixteen guards entered the room. They were fully armored; even the helmets covered their faces, making them look cold and lifeless. Then she let out a small gasp, the next man to enter the room was one she was hoping she'd never had to see again: Gahryn.

"You?!!" she yelled, trying to use her powers but nothing happened. "Oh, what do we have here? The maid that was conspiring with the two traitors, how quaint. Your powers won't work here, I have a special drug that will make sure of that," he smiled an evil smile. Lilah felt disgust. "What do you want from us, you murder, you traitor, you—," she called him every name under the sun, but he just waited patiently, smiling at her. "What a saucy tongue you have. Don't worry, we'll break that, won't we Penelope?" he said. "Y-yes, master," said a quivering voice. Lilah looked and her eyes widened. She barely recognized the former king's personal assistant. She had a weird look in her eyes, as if she'd seen a ghost, and hadn't stopped seeing it. She wore ragged clothing and had strange markings similar to the ones Yraviro had, on her neck and stomach, and seemed to extend to her privates. "What do I want? You, of course. I need more servants, and . . . . well you get the picture," Gahryn said, still smiling. Lilah hated that smile. They were strapped down. "Hey!! You can't do this!! I'm not property!! I'll kill you!! Just untie one hand and I'll kill you all!!" threatened Bazil. Gahryn chuckled, and pointed at Bazil, "Her first." A guard walked up with a rei rod and then—the door burst open. A guard in full armor stood there; then he threw his sword at the guard with the rei rod. Lilah gasped as she recognized the sword. The guard with the rei rod fell to the floor, dead. The guard took off his helmet and threw it at another guard. It was Jason. She heard a familiar charging voice and her jaw dropped as Dahrc entered the room, pummeling several guards. Dahrc was alive. She couldn't believe it. Her emotions were jumbled up with feelings of joy, anger, and just plain disbelieve.

Jason

Jason quickly removed the rest of his armor. He saw Lilah and Bazil, stripped and tied to iron tables with Gahryn next to them, a look of surprise upon his face. Out of the corner of his eye, he saw a shocking sight: Penelope. Gahryn had obviously had his way with her. Anger swelled within Jason as he picked up his sword and slew the remainder of the guards. As he was about to put his sword to Gahryn's neck, Gahryn drew his scythes and blocked, with speed matching Jason's. Dahrc freed the girls. "Jason? Why, isn't this a pleasant surprise? I've been looking for you," said Gahryn, in a silver voice. "What? What do you mean 'looking for me'?" Gahryn smiled. "Jason, son of Dihvr. Jason, renegade assassin, defected from the Aireni. Jason, the prodigy of the Aireni. Jason, the unbeatable. The pride of my organization. You are the one who could topple the gods!! You are my weapon!" A chill ran down Jason's neck. *Jason, the unbeatable.* That was what he was called in the Aireni, not that he cared for it, but no one except one in the Aireni would know it. *The pride of my organization.* This man wasn't in the Aireni, he ran it. He was the head master of the Aireni!! His identity was secret, so there wasn't any way Jason could have recognized him. "Y-You . . . . are the Headmaster of the Aireni?!"

Jason said, shocked. "Of course I am the Head master of the Aireni. You should—wait, you don't remember me? Oh I guess you wouldn't for you were three at the time. YOU ARE THE ONE WHO GAVE ME THIS!!" he said, pointing to his patched left eye, "It was supposed to be a lesson of humility for you, as all assassins learn, but instead YOU humiliated ME!! I admit I was mad at first, but then I realized just how skilled you are. Everything that has happened, the death of Dechur, the alliance with the Soul Eaters, all of it was so I could get my hands on you." He smiled a cruel smile, "But you didn't want to be controlled. You betrayed me and killed off even my most skilled servants! After I rebuilt the organization, I sent all of my best assassins, time after time, and still your skill was too much. I had lost hope, until you showed up after robbing the royal pantry." Jason stared in awe. But anger overwhelmed him, and then lunged, blade towards Gahryn's neck. Gahryn managed to block, the fight had begun. Jason jumped, spun, and brought his sword down towards Gahryn, but Gahryn moved out of the way, and struck quickly with his scythes. Jason parried and struck with a strong uppercut slash, Gahryn was only able to partially dodge, and Jason cut him on the forearm, but it was just a nick. Gahryn changed stances, and lunged with his scythes. Jason blocked one scythe, but Gahryn spun and slashed Jason across the cheek, and kicked him in the throat. Jason was sent to the wall, and upon impact, coughed up blood. Jason started to get back up, when he felt a sharp pain in his chest as Gahryn stabbed through his heart.

"JASON!!!" yelled Lilah, but it sounded distant, far away, everything began to slow down. *This can't be it*, thought Jason. But then Jason felt that calm again, and a smile touched his lips. Slowly, his head rose until he was eye to eye with Gahryn, still smiling. And all his hatred fused with the mysterious calm.   BooooooooWWWWWOOOOOOOOOOOOOO OOOOOOOOMMMMMMMM!!!!!!! An explosion of dark red aura emitted from Jason, throwing Gahryn back against the other wall. Withered, grey wings sprouted from his back, his hands changed, becoming clawed and iridescent, and upon seeing his reflection, his irises turned pale and shown with multicolor complexion. Dark markings surrounded his eyes. Then something different happened, the whites of his eyes turned blood red, his teeth sharpened mildly, and the music returned, more clearly than ever. Jason looked at everyone in the room, all of them with shock and fear in their eyes. He turned his attention to Gahryn, who had gotten back up. Dark red aura continued to emit from Jason, he smiled and said, "Gahryn, let's finish this, you shall pay for your crimes!" Gahryn attacked, and again Jason listened to the music. Gahryn's music was a quick, but profound melody with short and long notes, which struck long, enchanting chords as he maneuvered his scythes in perfect precision. Jason's melody resounded with chords of low and high octaves interchanging perfectly, with smooth notes that collided perfectly, a sound which, to Jason, sounded like heaven. And then melodies collided, making a harmony which put Jason into a deeper calm. Jason slashed, Gahryn tried to block but his scythes were cut in half and he was cut deeply across the chest, he only staggered, but remained standing. He charged, so did Jason. They collided and both flew out the window, breaking the glass. Gahryn began to chant and light started to swirl around him, as they started to fall to the ground. Jason used his wings to pull up. Gahryn's melody quickened and a rhythm of a heart beat joined it. Gahryn radiated with light, and wings made of the light spread out from Gahryn's back. They collided again, in mid air, in full view of the villagers and peasants of Durvyuria. Gahryn drew a knife and with the hilt, smashed Jason back into the castle. Gahryn laughed, "Is this, your best? It's GLORIOUS!!! Show me more!!" A savage, blood curling cry emitted from Jason, the castle began to shake violently. Jason emerged, but looked different; all traces of his human self gone. Gahryn's neck chilled in fear. Then faster than the eye could see, Jason tore Gahryn in half. Jason let loose a savage, yet beautiful roar. He was a beast of savageness and beauty. None could compare. Then thought returned to Jason. He looked into his reflection. He no longer looked human, his skin, a bluish iridescent color, from the corner of his mouth and up to his cheeks were two radiating, multicolored spikes, his teeth fully sharpened, his eyes were more slanted, and his body was armored like a skeletal dragon, complete with a lizard-like tail. He was truly terrifying, yet held more beauty than any diamond. Jason started to turn back, and while doing so he came closer to the ground. Before he touched the ground, Jason collapsed.

Lilah

Lilah looked at Dahrc. Gahryn's spells had been broken. She looked at Dahrc with untamed anger. "Lilah, I-I am sorry, it was Dechur's blood, it—," Dahrc started to say. "Don't. You betrayed us. You didn't just break my heart; you broke Jason's as well. Even if he doesn't show it. He had to kill you, YOUR BEST FRIEND HAD TO WATCH HIMSELF KILL YOU!! How could you do that? You and Jason were the only ones I have ever trusted, and YOU betrayed me," Lilah said, her heart beating painfully. "But I was—," Dahrc began to say, but Lilah stopped him. "I don't want to see you anymore; you caused pain not just to me, but Jason as well!! NOT MENTION YOU SLAUGHTERED ALL THOSE PEOPLE!!" Lilah paused, distraught. "Why?" she said, bursting into tears, "Why?" She turned back to him, and walked out of the castle.

Lilah looked for Jason, she didn't see him until she looked by the village fountain. Jason was lying face down on the ground. The villagers were hiding, not one in sight. "JASON!!" Lilah ran to him in worry. Yraviro was already there, but at a distance, as if terrified of Jason. Lilah rolled Jason over on his back. He still had the cut on his cheek and the wound in his chest. He wasn't breathing, and no pulse. "JASON!!! NO!!!! JASON!!!!" Lilah cried, shaking him, no response. "NO!! No! Oh gods no . . . . Jason! Get up!! Please!" Unending tears flowed from Lilah's eyes, when she heard a cough. She looked at Jason, he opened his eyes and said, "Is he still dead?" Lilah laughed and hugged really tight. "What do mean?" she asked, relieved that Jason was alive. ". . . . C . . . . Ca . . . . Can't breathe . . . . yer choking . . . ." Jason started to say. "Oh!! Sorry, sorry!!" Jason rubbed his neck, "Phew, that was—," Jason started to say. She kissed him. Slowly the villagers came out, unsure how to react. Jason laughed and said, "I was talking about Gahryn, is he still dead?" "Yes, he is. It—I—saw you kill him. He is dead, his soul has gone to the nether world," Yraviro said. They both stared at her. "You said 'I'. Hahaha, you actually said 'I'," said Jason. "Is it over?" a voice said. Lilah turned, it was Dahrc. "No, it isn't. There is still one thing needed to be done," said Jason. "What do you mean?" asked Dahrc. "I need to kill our father, or else we will never be free. I don't care what you have to say, I'm going anyways." A peasant girl walked up to Jason, she was no more than seven. "Here, mister, take this," she handed him a ring. Jason looked at her questioningly. "It's a teleport ring; it will help you get to Daterialiah." "How did you know I was going to Daterialiah?" asked Jason. "She is a seer, her words are always wise," an elder woman said, holding the little girl's hand. Jason started to put on the ring, "Wait. Let me come with you," said Dahrc, "He's my father too, so it is only right that I come as well." Jason nodded. Lilah looked at both of them, unreassuringly. Dahrc put his hand on Jason's shoulder and Jason put on the ring. They both vanished with a faint *wisp* sound.

CHAPTER 19

It's All in the Family

Jason

They appeared in the land of the gods. Dihvr was waiting for them. **"I knew you would be here Jason. After all I done, you still want to kill me? Who do you think brought Dahrc back? I was the one who asked Oros, the god of the Dead to bring him back. You are a fool if you think you can defeat me,"** Dihvr said in snide tone. Jason drew his sword. He wasn't looking for answers this time. The calm was still with him. But all anger was gone. He was in an odd peace, which he could not find the source. "I am calm. I didn't come here alone." Jason stepped aside, revealing Dahrc, full of rage. "YOU KILLED MY MOTHER!!" Dahrc seethed, drawing his axes. **"Hahahahahah!! Of course I did. She was weak. But I do not care to talk about her. However, YOU, Jason, do you feel that calm? Do you wonder where it comes from? It is your mother's ability. It is the**

reason I fell in love with her." Jason just stared at him, "As if a god of carnage could ever love, don't lie to me," Jason said, emotions quiet. Jason attacked first, using every muscle in his body to attack. Dahrc joined in, and it became a fight which finesse and strength battled against carnage. Jason blocked all of Dihvr's attacks. Dahrc attacked viciously, but all his attacks were blocked. Then the calm deepened, and Jason started to move at inhuman speeds, slashing Dihvr several times. Then, in no more than a second, Dihvr hit Jason to the ground, and at that very same instant, Dahrc leapt and plunged an axe into Dihvr's head. Dihvr laughed, and kept attacking. Jason got back up. Anger engulfed him, and with anger came memories, painful ones, which turned the anger into sheer hatred. Dihvr smiled as Jason transformed; another explosion of dark red aura. Jason attacked again, this time it was just him and his father. They clashed for several minutes, neither gaining any head way. Jason knew only one way to kill a god, without sending him to Nether world. So Jason faked a stab, twisted quickly and grabbed Dihvr. "Your Soul Shall Perish For Your Sins!!" Jason pulled out the god's soul and started to insert it into himself, which would make both of them perish, permanently. But at the last moment, before Jason could insert it, Dahrc shoved the soul within himself. "Dahrc? What are you doing?!!" Jason yelled. "I am doing what needs to done!! ARRRRGH!!! You have Lilah, you can't lose her! You are my friend; I don't want you to be like me! This is the only way I can make up for my sins!! AAAARRRRRGHHH!!! AAHHHH!!! His soul may be gone, but his body isn't! You have to kill Dihvr while he is soul-less! AAHHHH—," Dahrc said, then he exploded in a dark energy, and everything went silent.

Jason turned and looked at Dihvr; anger, sorrow, determination, and most shockingly, calmness enveloped inside of Jason. Jason charged, they clashed again. But it was different this time for Jason, it was as if Dihvr had slowed down, and it seemed as if nothing but him and Dihvr moved, everything else seemed to stand still. Then in one powerful, emotion infused slash, Jason cut through Dihvr's circular blade and cut across the chest. Jason was no longer in his awakened form, he was human again. "That was for my sister!!" he yelled. Jason kicked his father in the face and slashed again, making an "X" across his chest. "THAT WAS FOR MY MOTHER!!!" he said, getting louder and fiercer. Pulled Dalia's scythe from the loop in his belt, jumped, and underhandedly stabbed the blade into Dihvr's heart. "**THAT WAS FOR DALIA!!!**" He kicked Dihvr in the throat, jumped back using the recoil, and drew his sword. He jumped high, brought the sword into Dihvr's head. "THAT WAS FOR DAHRC!!!" Jason bellowed, anger increasing. **"ARHHHHH!!!! NO!! I WILL NOT DIE!!!"** Dihvr, tried to attack, Jason dodged and jumped into the air, and flipped six times before bringing his foot down on his sword, which was lodged in Dihvr's skull. *"**AND THIS IS FOR LILAH!!!!!!**"* An explosive shockwave resonated from the impact, the ground shook, the clouds dispersed; debris flew for miles on end. Then it was over. Jason stood there, panting, as he looked upon the shattered dead body of Dihvr. Dalia's scythe had shattered, and expecting the same, he looked at his sword. It was embedded in the ground, with the hilt standing perfectly straight. Jason walked over to it, and wrapped one hand around the handle. He pulled once, it didn't budge. He pulled again, and this time it came out. Jason couldn't believe his eyes. His mother's sword was in perfect condition. Tears flooded from his eyes, but he uttered not a word. Then he slipped on the teleport ring, and he was gone.

Lilah

Jason came back, but Dahrc wasn't with him. Dalia's scythe was missing as well. Jason walked over to Lilah and, surprising her, kissed her. Jason seemed to lose it. He collapsed to his knees and cried, hard. It was a silent cry, full of pain, sorrow, and relief. Lilah felt like tormentor when she asked, "Where's Dahrc? What happened?" Jason seemed to gather himself, and when he spoke, he seemed distant, "We met our father. We fought, and I was . . . . different. I took out Dihvr's soul; I was going to plant it into myself, making Dihvr mortal, but I would perish forever, no netherworld. And Dahrc . . . . he took the soul instead. He said it was his atonement for his sins. He said that I shouldn't leave you, that I shouldn't become like him. He's gone . . . ." Jason paused, as his emotions changed, "Then I killed Dihvr. He wouldn't die, Dahrc had lodged an axe into his skull, but Dihvr kept going. I don't know how, but the calm—it was complete.

I killed him in the name of my mother, my sister, Dalia, Dahrc . . . ." there was a momentary paused as he looked into her eyes, ". . . . and you." She hugged Jason until the sun had set. Jason was offered the crown, but he refused, saying, "I am many things, a monster, a man, a murderer, a savior, even a Soul Eater/Human/god, but I am no king. I am no king." Jason, Lilah, Bazil, Yraviro, and Penelope walked towards the city gates. Penelope decided she would take the crown, and restore beauty and power to Durvyuria. Bazil asked to travel with Jason and Lilah, so she could find her mother and sister. And Yraviro became the first Soul Eater to help the humans in the Soul Eater and Human war. Lilah looked at Jason. "Are you okay?" she asked him. He smiled, "I don't know, we've lost so much. I've lost my mother, my sister, Dalia, and even my only brother that I didn't know I had. But at least there are some good things. You, Gahryn's death, Dihvr's downfall, and finally, I will get to be a father." They both chuckled. She rested her head on his shoulder as they began their next adventure, with hopes of new happiness.

CHAPTER 20

Epilogue

And so, Jason and Lilah had their child, a daughter, which they named Dariah in honor of Dahrc and Dalia. Penelope turned out to be a powerful queen after Gahryn's death. Six years later she found herself a king, which treated her kindly and with respect. Yraviro learned self confidence, and she fell in love with a human. Bazil separated from Lilah and Jason after a few years, and disappeared.

Jason and Lilah disappeared as well, all that was found were scorch marks and blood, but no bodies, and Dariah wrapped up in a blanket, hidden with Jason's sword. But that is a tale for another time.

And so, I, King Dechur, hope that someone finds this journal and remember the true heroes of this Nation, these are my final words.

King Dechur.

"Your Majesty, what are you doing? Don't you have to select an heir?" asked Penelope. "Sorry,

Penelope, I was having another premonition." I responded. "And writing it down in this . . . . what is this?" she asked. "Nothing." I chuckled. Sir, shouldn't you prepare, you know, your age in years is nearing its peak." "Atlas Penelope, you and Gahryn both know I hold no heir to the throne. So thus the decision is up to me to who ascends the throne. I specifically sta—," Two of my guards entered the room.

"Your Majesty, we have two prisoners here that have been accused of thievery, by Sir Fareld," said the leftwing guard. "That man is always causing trouble, if it weren't for his heroic deeds at the March of Durvyuria, I would have him strung up and whipped for insolence. Huuuh, oh well. What is it?"

Two boys were dragged in, followed by a housemaid I didn't recognize. The boys kept their heads low and the maid just watched them. "My lord," the maid curtsied.

"Hmmm," I said, "These two boys and you my dear, share destinies."

The maid blushed, "Is that so, My Lord?" "'Tis is true for I have seen it, though how they are linked eludes me . . . . Might I ask you your name?"

"Yes, My Lord, I am Lilah, Irea and Mescov's daughter."

PRONUNCIATIONS

This is to help fellow readers with pronouncing tough words and names, I hope you enjoyed my book and look forward to its sequel. The language used in the book is closely English, but some names have a different pronunciation than first thought.

Aireni—(Ā-REN-eye)   **Yraviro**—(Yuh-RAHV-iR-ŏh)
Arstas—(AR-stás)
Bahyrnheit—(Bah-hurn-hite)
Bazil—(BĀ-zeel)
Dahrc—(Dark)
Dalia—(Dä-LEAH)
Daterialiah—(Dah-TEER-REE-al-LEAH)
Dechur—(Deh-ch-urr)
Dihvr—(Dih-vurr)
Durvyuria—(DERR-VeeYur-EAH)
Erale—(Ee-Ray-el)
Fareld—(Far-eeld)
Gahryn—(Gah-REN)
Granisti—(Gra-n-est-ee)
Gravre—(Grah-vurr)

Jason—(Jay-sohn)
Lilah—(Lye-luh)
Pelea—(Peh-leah)
Penelope—(puh-nel-uh-pee)